I0720871

ISBN-ebook: 978-1-945519-13-0
ISBN-Print: 978-1-945519-15-4
Cover art by Pyscat Studios
Interior artwork by Cory Tilton
www.elizatilton.com
Give feedback on the book at:
info@elizatilton.com

First Edition
Printed in the U.S.A

"Wherever you know of harm, regard that harm as your own;
and give your foes no peace"
~Odin, Havamal 197.

1

The dire wolf stayed by my side, growling at the strange mist hovering over the sleeping Slav settlement. Wind, smelling of scorched earth, howled around our ragged band, swirling the fog by our feet. The cold dampness of night clung to my clothes, and I was grateful for the fur-lined cape. Our torches cut through the darkness, revealing several log homes, the earth around them burnt black, ready for planting.

"Easy, Fey," I said, patting the wolf's head.

Vega, my father's second, yawned and stretched out his arms as we walked. "Twelve days of traveling and this is where we land?" He shook his head. "Better have some good mead or I'm walking back to Kiev."

"We'll find rest for tonight," my father said. "Tomorrow we shall put an end to these rumors of the undead."

A chill settled in my bones. Stories of Vikings rising from the ground had traveled from the western shores of the Dnieper River. We followed the tales south, traveling past the great city of Kiev to this eastern homeland. We should have returned home, back to our people, but when your chieftain sends orders, there is no disobeying.

"Rurik wouldn't have sent us here if he thought otherwise," I said.

Father nodded, and Vega grunted, seeming annoyed by this whole trip.

Ragna and Flo, our other companions who scouted ahead, whistled us forward, pointing to the longhouse at the top of the small hill. A stream of smoke puffed out the top of the thatched roof. No Slavs walked around this night, and when we entered the longhouse there were few to greet us.

"Stay here," I ordered Fey, and he found a spot next to the entrance to lie down.

A fire roared in the center of the room with three older men sitting around the pit. They passed a long wooden pipe between them and glared at our arrival, one gripped the axe at his side. Ratty clothes draped across them, the shredded linen blending with the gray of their beards.

"Are you from Novgorod?" A girl with cream skin and shadowy-brown eyes stepped toward my father.

"Aye," Father said. "I am Holmgeirr; this my son Folkvarr, Vega, Ragna, and Flo. Rurik sent us to investigate the rumors."

"We had heard of your coming arrival." She pointed to the white-haired man sitting in between the other two. "Juri is our leader. The men on his sides are Belbog and Dragon."

Juri smoked from the pipe and nodded.

"I am Danica. I'll bring you something to eat." The girl disappeared behind the bear furs hanging to our right, and we each found a spot by the fire.

Juri puffed on the pipe, letting out long wisps of smoke. "So you've come from the North." His haggard face showed many winter years, and his white hair reminded me of bones left in ash. "I'm sorry you wasted your time," he said.

Vega and my father exchanged a glance. "The rumors are false?" Vega asked.

"Of course they are false," Belbog said. His fat cheeks were red and he guzzled from a horn. "Walking dead . . . " He laughed and specks of mead splashed on his already dirty beard.

My companions and I did not share his humor. Whether true or false, the claims being made against our brethren were blasphemous. I dug my fingers into my wool trousers, clenching the fabric. Smoke hazed the air, making my eyes burn. Did they know nothing about honor and death? To die, and never reach the halls of Valhalla? My mouth filled with saliva and I bit back the urge to spit at their feet.

The Slavs were known for their hatred of our kind. Even after the raids diminished and fair trade took its place, the hatred lived on. I could feel the disgust in the way they sneered at our dress and cursed behind our backs. Truth would never be given freely with them.

They couldn't be trusted.

Danica returned carrying wooden bowls filled with porridge and handed one to each of us. I brought the bowl to my nose, sniffing the mushrooms, nothing poisonous, but not appetizing either. I yearned for Mother's nettle soup after our long journey.

"You may rest here tonight," Juri said. "And tomorrow you can see for yourselves."

My father looked at me with a slight nod—my order to rest first. I had my fill of the salted porridge and I leaned back against the log seat. The quiet conversation turned to the great Kiev. Viking and Slav alike had interest in the city and trade taking place. Soon, many more would come to see its rising glory. I closed my eyes, dreaming of the sea. The rushing waves churning like a beast and roaring against the ship. It had been too many years since we had been to the homeland. The sooner we left here, the sooner we could complete our journey and finally return home.

Father nudged me awake. I opened my eyes, surprised how easily I'd fallen asleep. Vega had already rolled to his side, blade near his chest which heaved up and down with sleep. The two other men who were here when I first arrived had disappeared. Juri sat across from us, still puffing on a pipe.

"Where are Ragna and Flo?" I asked.

Father titled his head to the side where I followed his gaze to Flo who whispered to the girl Danica. The grimace on her face spoke a thousand words, and I grinned. Flo did not care what type of woman you were, only that you found him appealing. Though with his shaved head, and the black markings covering it, many cringed at his presence. Flo plucked a rune stone from his trousers, one of the many trinkets he carried, and placed it in the girl's hand.

"Ragna found sleep outside. Go with him. Flo will watch here."

"Are you sure?"

"Go." My father watched Flo, but shifted into a more relaxed position. Though his eyes were open, I knew he rested. He was one of the few men I knew who could sleep with open eyes. I found it a bit unnerving.

My bones cracked as I stood and stretched out my arms. Seventeen winters, old enough to battle, but too young for aching joints. I needed a run.

I preferred the watch before dawn: the hour of the gods. Fey and I waited outside the longhouse as dawn began to grace us with her presence. No one in the village had woken yet. We were in a small settlement with crops that smelled of scorched earth and an eerie mist that hovered over everything.

This quest was madness. I wanted to fight, not walk around these lands following a story, especially one that would prove false. Before Rurik sent us here, we were scouting west of the river. A group of rebellious Slavs were stirring trouble and needed to be dealt with. We would have arrived within days if Rurik hadn't sent word to re-direct our path. Now, we would be stuck here even longer.

I kicked at a stone in the dirt, dislodging it, and sending it down the hill.

Fey trotted away from me, most likely to hunt. Normally, I would go with him, but I couldn't leave Father and the rest of our group without a watch.

The wooden door to a longhouse on the far right opened and a girl walked out carrying a bucket. A white scarf covered her hair, secured by bronze temple rings on each side. The long red dress she wore swayed against the dirt. The blood red color contrasted against the white apron she wore over it. Our gazes met across the hazed ground, and I stood straighter. Her mouth turned into a frown.

I don't want to be here either.

2

What was a Viking doing here? What business did they have in our land? My heart did a fast thump as I briskly walked into the forest. The sun hovered low, barely breaching the thick foliage. Most of the forest slept, leaving me alone with my thoughts.

The last time I saw a Viking was the day my parents died.

No, died was too kind of a word, murdered was better.

We were a little homestead, nothing worth conquering, yet they had come in the black of night. Raping, murdering, and burning almost everything to the ground. Yaya had taken my sister and me into the woods to protect us, but she couldn't protect us from the memories of seeing our parents slaughtered by barbarians.

My chest tightened, and I shook the fear away. It was three years ago and times had changed. The Vikings settled in Kiev and Novgorod, and peace filtered throughout the lands. I wouldn't be afraid. Not anymore.

I walked to the well and hooked the bucket onto the levy and lowered the rope.

The tune of Mama's favorite hymn entered in my mind, and I hummed the melody.

At this hour, I would see foxes and squirrels busing away, woodpeckers pecking at the trees, yet I saw none. I heard none.

"I bet you're all scared of the barbarians too." The forest didn't respond to me so I continued with my morning duties.

The bucket splashed into the water, and I began pulling it back up, gazing around at the mist. Kievan mist always swam through our lands. Some of our people believed the mist to be a sentient being, and one that angered when her lands were toyed with. I found comfort within the gray fog. It reminded me of a mother's warm blanket wrapped around her children, keeping them tight to her bosom. Mist swirled around my toes, and I lifted my foot into it. I had left my shoes at home, preferring the soft grass against my feet.

When the bucket reached the top, I unhooked it, and pulled it off. Water splashed the wooden rim, and I repositioned the bucket in between both hands. Still humming, I stepped away from the well, and turned toward home. Danica would return from Juri's soon and I wanted to prepare fresh porridge for her.

A strange coldness tickled my neck. The tiny hairs covering my body straightened and my heart beat wildly. I had never been afraid of the forest. It has always been a sanctuary, even when the leshie thought it was fun to steal my bread and hide my kerchief—I learned to never leave anything unattended in the woods. The woodland spirits loved playing games.

"Not today," I warned the leshie. "Or I'll send the

chuhaister after you." A smile played on my lips. I had no idea how to contact the forest giant, and I had never seen him, still, the little tricksters didn't know that.

Wind whooshed into my back, sending my rubaKHa and kerchief flapping forward. I gripped the bucket with my left hand while I fixed myself with the other. The bottom red linen of my rubaKHa tinged brown. Too many days running in the forest with not enough washing in between.

Hssssss.

I glanced around at the trees, searching for the peculiar noise.

My head yanked back. I fell backward onto the ground as something grabbed my hair and dragged me across the dirt. The temple rings came loose and the kerchief slipped off my scalp.

"Help!" I clawed at sinewy hands holding my hair in a tight grip. I twisted back and forth as the tall pines passed by me in a flash. My neck burned, and my thrashing did nothing to slow the monster's pace.

Scratching at the hands, I craned my neck back, trying to see what attacked me, but I flipped over, the creature walking too fast for me to see anything.

Fear clenched my throat, turning my scream into a hoarse yell.

I fumbled for the dagger I kept in my apron pocket. I rolled over, again, and my head slammed into a nearby tree. Blood trickled from the cut and ran into my right eye, blinding and dazing me. Where was this thing taking me? What was taking me? My mind whirred with horror stories of monsters in the woods, all silly childhood tales too terrifying to believe.

Think. Think. Think.

Taking a deep breath to calm myself, I grabbed the dagger, and drove the blade above my head and into the creature's hands.

Nothing.

Not a cry. Not a moment of hesitation. It was as if the cut didn't even hurt it!

The creature twisted his hand and ripped off my head scarf to grip my hair tighter.

I wasn't strong, or a good fighter, but I could run. If I could get free, I could try to outrun whatever had me.

Tears blurred my vision, and grabbed a chunk of my hair right below the creature's hands. With my other hand, I brought the blade to my hair and sawed it off. My head smashed on the ground, and before the creature could turn and attack, I jumped to my feet and ran. Heavy steps chased me, but I kept running and never once looked back at the monster behind me.

<h1 style="text-align:center">3</h1>

Dampness coated the ground and stuck to my skin. I itched to be gone from this place and back toward our home in Novgorod. We stood in front of the longhouse, Juri and his men urging us to return to Rurik with 'all is well'.

"There's nothing here, Holmgeirr." Vega stretched out his neck. "Let's go. This place stinks."

Juri and his men had shown us the village, pigs, goats, a few crops, some barns, nothing else. But my father sensed something. He *always* sensed something. Sometimes I wondered if Odin's ravens whispered in his ear. My father squinted at the distance, searching the mist.

Flo and Ragna returned from their scouting. "Nothing past the hills," Flo said.

"Or south of the river," Ragna finished. "There's nothing here."

"Then we go." My father swung his battle-axe back into the holder on his back. He glanced over at Juri. "We will tell Rurik we found nothing, but if we hear word of dead Vikings in this land again, you will answer for it."

Juri nodded. "Understood. Send Rurik our regards."

Fey's hair stood at attention, the fur on his mane expanding outwardly, making him look even fiercer than he already was. Baring his teeth, the mighty dire wolf growled and dashed forward.

Screams came from the north, and I chased after Fey. A girl crashed out of the nearby woods. Blood smeared her pale face. I recognized her from this morning.

"Agna!" Danica shoved past me and grabbed the girl around her slender frame. They both fell to the ground in a heap.

"What happened?" She pushed Agna's hair back, inspecting the wound. The girl's handkerchief and temple rings were missing. Her long blonde hair knotted against her shoulders, and it looked shorter than this morning.

"In the forest . . . a creature."

Father's jaw clenched. He stomped down the hill to where the girls sat, slinging the battle-axe out. "What kind of creature?"

Agna shook her head. Blood covered the right side of her face and her hands shook. "I don't know. I couldn't see. It was . . . dragging me."

"Oh, Agna." Danica hugged her then took her hand, helping her stand.

"Can you show us?" I asked.

Agna gawked at me. "I can't go back there."

"You'll be safe with us." I tried to reassure her, but fear filled her bright green eyes.

"My sister is hurt. She's not going anywhere." Danica pulled Agna away, glaring at us as she left.

"Which direction did the creature come from?" my father yelled at them.

Agna pointed a shaky hand north. "Straight, until you see the well."

With an agreed nod, we dodged into the woods, running past large fir trees and crushing the earth in our wake. Within moments, the stone well appeared through the mist.

Fey snarled, revealing his deadly fangs as he growled beside me.

"I sense it too." I slipped out both my axes from their side sheaths, one for each hand. Quietly, I stepped, heel to toe, remaining on the outer edge of my boots, creeping low as I made my way forward. My breath became visible in the air. The temperature drop was unusual for this time of year. Winter still had a few more months before she came. I knelt, inspecting the grass around my feet.

"Here." Father pointed to the flattened brush.

Blood dotted the area by a tree and smeared the grass past the well.

"I see tracks." Flo called out. "Deeper into the woods."

We stormed through the woods, chasing after the uneven tracks. I almost ran into Vega when he stopped short. Rain fell from the sky, mudding the ground. Gray skies shadowed above us, blocking out the earlier rays of dawn.

"By the gods . . ."

A man sat on the ground, drinking from the neck of a deer. His skin tinged gray with rings of purple around his eyes. Long hair hung off his scalp in patches, and his face reminded me of haunted nightmares. Noticing our approach, he jumped with surprising speed and launched at Vega with wild hands. Without hesitation, Vega, a seasoned combatant, met the creature with an axe to the chest. "He is no Viking, but he's not alive either!"

The undead ripped himself off the wedged blade as if it were a simple stick. Blood leaked from the wound. It grinned, a toothy-eyed smile, then ran.

"After it!" Father yelled.

From the side brush, four more nightmarish aberrations charged at us with crude looking swords coated in rust. Loud gurgling screams coursed from their gaping mouths. I leapt at the one closest to me. A festering hole remained where his left eye should be, but he moved as if he needed no sight at all. Twirling my axes, I ducked low and rushed in, leading with a right-handed horizontal swipe. He blocked my blow with a large broadsword, rust sparking into a small cloud as the blades met. For a man who didn't look alive, he fought with wit.

Fey bit at his leg, but the creature ignored the wolf and swung his sword at me in a wide arc, dragging the massive beast as it relentlessly pressed forward. Swiftly ducking the jagged blade, I countered with a deep backhand slice across his hamstring. The hit was deep and would have stopped most men, but the creature pressed on. Rising back to a fighting stance, I spun in a pirouette, barely evading its vicious downward chop. The blade was so close that it brushed against the hairs of fur draped over the back of my shoulders, strands of the pelt danced on the current of wind. Completing my rotation, I used my body's momentum to send two horizontal strikes at the creatures exposed right flank. High and low, my axe swiftly drove home, one severing his right arm off at the elbow, and the other driving deeply into the side of its skull. Torquing my wrist, I removed the axe from the grievous head wound, and the abomination twitched as it fell lifeless to the ground.

In front of me stood the three-remaining attackers, black knot patterns covered one of the undead man's hands and traveled up his forearms—markings of a Viking. Water dripped off his haggard face, and in his gaze, I saw emptiness.

Behind him two more in similar fashion, pressed in. Fey hit the creature to the far right, high and fast. The monster's attention was on me and he never saw the low flying ball of teeth, claws and fur, which tackled him from the rear. Powerful jaws gnashed into the flesh of the man's neck. Thrashing his head wildly, Fey snapped the creature's spine as it removed its head completely, then darted back into the woods with his latest trophy.

Moving on instinct, I went to engage the man in front of me in the melee, but was stopped dead in my tracks. A hand wrapped around my neck, pulling me back onto my heels.

My father's axe flew past my face, so close it nicked the top of my ear. The grip on my neck eased and fell away. I turned to see his trusted old axe stuck in another undead man's head.

"Move," Father ordered. "More are coming from the woods."

Savagely, he barreled into the creature still stalking toward me. His powerful frame shouldering right through the creature, sending him face first into the muddy earth below.

Nodding, I quickly delivered the coup de grace, to the back of the prone creature's skull, while Father retrieved his axe.

Six of the undead surrounded Ragna and Flo. Vega fought against three. Shadows moved around the trees, figures in dark cloaks. If I was to die this day, it would be a warrior's death and Odin himself would greet me into the gates.

Father and I charged the oncoming wave, hacking through the oncoming swarm, trying to reach our companions. Giving the old man room was both wise and advantageous; he resembled a wild grizzly. Blow after blow he swept into their ranks, screaming as if possessed by death itself. Not every strike was a killing blow, though more were than not. He hewed through them as if they were old wine skins. Body parts flew in a flurry of deadly strikes as he swung with reckless abandon.

I stayed to his back, guarding his flanks. Dodging and weaving in and out of strikes, I finished off the wounded attackers lucky enough to survive the initial encounter with my father. Even with the wounds they received, strikes that would drop a bear, these abominations pressed on. The only killing blow seemed to be one that pierced the skull and struck the brain, that or decapitation.

Bodies piled up around us, but we had yet to gain any ground as more came.

Two slipped past my father's deadly assault, and were approaching me from either side, rushing in quickly. Perpendicular to them both, my head swiveled as I tried to keep both in my line of sight. They coordinated their strikes perfectly and came in with twin horizontal sweeps intended to scissor me in half. I had never been more thankful for the training my father put me through. So many times I had thought him cruel, and unrealistic in the limits to which he would push me to. Today, I understood why he pushed me so hard.

I met both strikes with perfectly timed parries, my left-hand low and behind me, my right hand high and holding the blade off in front. We were in a standstill, and I couldn't shift an inch, or I would expose myself. Exhaustion filled my limbs, and it took all my strength to stay on the defensive.

The familiar growl of my four-legged best friend reminded me I wasn't alone. Swift as a bolt of lightning from Thor's Hammer, Fey streaked across the battlefield and slammed into the creature to my right. His blood-soaked mouth sinking deep into the rotted calf of the stunned assailant—the strike ripped the creature's leg clean off at the knee cap. As quickly as Fey had entered the fight, he ran off again, the monster's torn leg locked in its jaws.

As the monster to my right fell away, releasing me from holding the parry, I quickly turned with my free weapon and sliced down with pure rage. Fury can carry a man far. My father would often say my anger was a gift from Thor. Well, I put as much as I could into that strike, and took both the creature's hands in the process. Its sword was still falling to the earth as I crossed my arm and delivered twin scissor strikes of my own, sending the monster's head to join the sword in the blood-soaked earth.

A burning ached in my muscles, and the axes I held became so very heavy. Stiffness in my arms made it hard to maneuver. My feet slid on the wet earth, and my father grabbed the back of my coat, standing me upright.

Mud and blood mixed with one another. Fatigue pulsed

through my body and my swings became less accurate. This was the end, but it would be a good death.

As the dark clouds and rain stopped, morning light filtered through the forest. The nightmare men began to retreat into the darkness of the woods until they were all gone.

Panting, I rested my hands on my thighs, searching for Fey. He came out of the woods completely covered in red, blood caked and matted his fur. My gaze landed on Vega who knelt by Ragna who lay silent, a deep gash across his chest.

The Slavs had lied.

4

watched the Northmen head into the forest, our forest. While my heart still thumped wild from the strange attack, the thought of those Vikings storming through the woods sent a frightening shiver down my spine, bringing back the memories and fear of that monstrous night, so long ago. While I learned to live without the comfort of our parents, the vision of blood scattering their broken bodies still haunted my dreams.

Danica guided me to the chair. "Sit. I'll get some water."

"It's because of *them*," she said, taking linen from the shelf and dumping it into the basin bowl. "The wood spirits are angry."

As she shook her head and cursed the Northmen who had stolen so much, my mind wandered to the woods. Woods I loved and played in since I could run with the mist beneath my toes. The strange *hissing* sound from the creature reminded me of death and mourning, pain, suffering, a hundred emotions wrapped up in a single note.

The sinewy hands . . . hands . . . They were human hands!

"Ouch!" I flinched as Danica pressed the wet cloth against my forehead and wiped away the blood.

"You'll need to be stitched." She touched my head softer.

"It was human."

"What was?" Danica dropped the cloth into the basin and walked to our herb chest.

"The creature." I hugged myself, coldness seeping into my bones. I desperately wanted the dirt off my arms and legs, the brush out of my tangled hair. "I need to bathe." I stood, bright spots blurred my vision and the ground swayed.

"Hold still, sister." Danica grabbed my waist. "I'll heat the water. The tub still has the water from last night. After the Northmen arrived, I never had a chance to come home and bathe."

I sat back down and stared at my shaking hands. *Human hands. But they were so cold and clammy.* "What if the rumors are true? What if . . . what if the *dead* walk?"

"You are starting to sound like them," she huffed, and crushed klamath weed into the mortar, her dark eyes full of fire.

Our parents' death had hardened her. The sweet, happy girl I once chased pigs with had matured into our mama and worried about everything. The harsh reality of our loss stole her innocence, an innocence I missed dearly. I prayed to the gods she would return to the young girl who found beauty in an earthworm. Being the older sister, it was my job to protect Danica, to help her see the hope in this difficult world and prove our parents' death did not mean ours.

Danica placed a steaming cup on the table. "Here, drink this." She pushed it toward me. I was so lost in my thoughts I hadn't realized she'd brewed tea.

I sipped the warm drink, letting it coat my parched throat. Rain fell outside blanketing the morning in dark clouds. Tiny drops slipped through the hole in the roof. I knew I should have replaced the sod after the last storm.

Our Aunt Jasna continued to pester us about leaving this place and living with her in Kiev, but we were protected here. Yaya would never leave her hut in the woods, and since she was our wise woman, our people saw that we were well looked after.

Papa built this home. How could we leave it?

"Are you ready?"

I nodded at Danica then pushed the empty cup away. My muscles relaxed as the tea worked its way into my body. This wasn't the first time I'd needed stitches. When I was five, I had played swords with a boy, and after I jabbed his side with the wooden weapon, he pushed me down and my elbow smacked onto a rock and split open.

Porridge spilled across the dirt floor by my feet. "Did you forget to salt the porridge again?" If we didn't over salt the porridge, Grandfather, our house spirit, would knock over the bowl and make a mess.

"No. I added a pinch. I can't eat it with all that salt."

We had never actually seen Grandfather, but the missing items and knocked over bowls were all clues to his peculiar existence. With our parents no longer here to keep him at bay, even our barley stores were at risk of being scattered around our home.

I bit my lip as the needle pierced my skin, and tried to not think about this morning. I would need to visit Yaya soon. She would know what creatures might be lurking in our woods. The spirits always seemed akin to her, whispering answers and long tales into her ears.

"There." Danica sat back and patted my forehead with the damp cloth soaked in klamath weed. "You only needed four today. That may be your smallest scar yet."

I ran my finger across the cut, feeling the thread sewn in right above my brow.

Danica took the pot off the stone oven nestled in the corner of the room, and dumped the steaming water into the wooden tub, then whirled it around with a big stick. "It's ready."

I untied my apron and slipped out of my clothes. Bumps rose on my arms from the cold draft, and I quickly stepped into the tub. Hot water seeped into my skin, and my muscles loosened. I sighed and sank deeper into the water, relaxing my head back on the wooden rim. Danica took a comb and began to brush the knots out of my hair.

"Your hair is.. Did you cut it?"

"I had to."

She leaned over and kissed the top of my head. "Everything will be okay. You'll see. You needed a cut anyway. Your hair grows too fast."

I smiled at her. Danica kept her hair just past her shoulders while I preferred mine long, all the way to my bottom. Now, my beautiful blonde locks only touched the middle of my back.

Closing my eyes, I tried to enjoy the warm water.

Baths were a luxury. It took too many trips to the river to bring the water back. Most of our people bathed in the river, but Mama had a strange obsession with cleanliness. She could never stand to see dirt on her hands and spent many nights scrubbing her fingernails until her fingers were red. Papa had built a wooden tub for our home and filled it once a week for us, even though he preferred the cold rush of river water.

With each stroke of the brush, drowsiness caressed my limbs. I hugged my legs to my chest and rested my head against them. Danica hummed, filling the room with Mama's melody. The warmth sent me to sleep and I prayed to Perun that I would not be haunted by ghoulish memories, or the creeping, harrowing, hissing from today.

5

Vega carried Ragna over his shoulder as we sloshed across the sodden earth back to the Slavs. Father walked in front of us, leading the march. His brown furs glistened from the rain. Anger swirled around us all, and I refused to acknowledge the fear that clawed at my mind.

How was this act of the gods possible? Would they allow one of their own to return from the dead? No, that could never be. To die in honor meant eternity in Valhalla. These creatures would never walk through that glorious door.

Flo rapped his sword against his shield. I slid my own shield off my back and tapped one of my axes against it; the sound reverberated through the air and through me. Our loud thumps caused the doors of the nearest homes to open and for the Slavs to peek outside. I ignored the stares. Instead, I focused on the rage, still high from the battle, and the loss of our brother.

Juri and his two men stood outside the longhouse staring at us as we walked up the hill.

"You lied," Father said.

"We—"

My father swung his axe and Juri's head fell to the ground, stopping him from speaking any more. His comrades cowered, weapons hiding in their scabbards.

Father turned around and addressed the people filling the area. "I am now your leader. We will discover who has been practicing these black arts and raising the dead. Follow our orders and you will all live."

None of the Slavs spoke, but the tears and angry sneers said enough. We had killed their leader, taken their settlement, and they could do nothing. With Rurik leading the northern lands, the Slavs had to abide by his rules.

"Juri!"

The girl from the woods ran forward. Her wet straw-colored hair hung loose and she covered her mouth with her shaking hands. The cut on her head had been stitched.

"Why would you do this?" she yelled. "We have done nothing!"

Flo spun around and pointed his sword tip in her direction. "Hush girl."

"You." Father pointed to her. "What is your name?"

"Agna."

"You will serve us in there." He pointed to Juri's longhouse.

Her mouth opened then clamped shut.

"No, Agna!" Danica ran up beside her.

Agna touched her arm. "I'll be fine. Go check on Yaya. Make sure those creatures haven't gone near her home."

Danica nodded and hugged her goodbye.

Agna held her chin high in the air and followed my father inside.

Vega laid Ragna on the floor of the longhouse. I wondered how we could perform a proper ritual so far from home. Who would go with him to Valhalla? And with no Angel of Death, how would the rites be done?

Flo clamped a hand on my shoulder. "What troubles you? This is a happy day."

"Nothing. Just wondering what smells so bad in here."

He laughed and tapped my shoulder before wandering off.

Father sat in the wooden chair in front of the fire. His blank expression gave nothing to his thoughts. Agna brought him a horn and he grabbed her arm. "Prepare a feast and bring women."

Agna's eyes widened and I thought she would talk back; instead, she handed him the horn and met his gaze. "I'll need to leave to find Juri's servants. They may be at another house, unsure of their place." Her words were even, but her hands trembled.

"Go quickly."

Though I should have been rejoicing with my brothers, I found no joy in what transpired in the woods. How could the dead walk?

"Why the long face?" Flo handed me a horn sloshing with mead.

I took the horn from his hands, but made no attempt to drink. "Those were not men."

"Aye. Devils." He slugged back the mead.

"Dead men . . ." Vega shook his head. "How is this possible?"

We looked to my father, the oldest and wisest man either

of us knew. My father had battled since his arms were strong enough to wield an axe. He gazed into the fire, holding his horn. Deep lines creased his forehead as he thought before responding. "This land is full of dark spirits and magic. Someone has created this."

"Who? And where did those Vikings come from? I thought we were the closest to Kiev? Isn't that why Rurik sent us?" The questions rambled out of my mouth. I couldn't grasp how any of this was possible.

"Vikings have traveled here before, and many make their way from Novgorod to Kiev," Father said. "It could be stragglers, or traders. Either way they must be put to rest."

"Aye." We all nodded.

Agna returned with three women: one who carried a basket of vegetables, and two who smiled weakly, and approached us by the fire. Agna had put the white scarf back on her head, and secured it with the bronze temple rings. Our gazes met and she lifted her chin high as she asked my father what else he required.

While Vega flirted with the two women, I watched Agna. How her tone showed respect, yet a fire brimmed beneath her words. Her hands bunched the apron she wore. As if she sensed my sight on her, she glanced to the side.

I quickly turned my head away and guzzled the drink.

"Tell me what you know about the undead men." Father's question stirred my curiosity. Would she be truthful or lie to protect her people.

Agna sat on the log across from me, her bright green gaze meeting mine. "There have been stories of men dying in a drunken state and not passing on or someone who wasn't buried properly tormenting their relatives at night, but in all my seventeen years I have never seen such a thing."

"Men do not just walk out of their graves," Vega said. "Do you have a soothsayer here or one who might know more about these creatures?"

Agna clenched the front of her dress, and refused to look away from the fire.

Flo slid his hand across her shoulders. She flinched at his sudden closeness, and tried to slide away from him. Flo grabbed her neck. "Speak girl."

"My grandmother," she croaked. Her widened eyes glistened.

"And where is she?" Flo spoke softly, but Agna tensed as he leaned closer.

I had traveled with him long enough to know his less than honorable methods. If she did not answer, he would force the words out.

Tell him.

"In the forest."

He slid his hand to her waist, and whispered in her ear. "Show me."

"I'll go." I stood.

Flo glared at me with a sly grin on his face. I don't know why I said that, only that the urge to see Flo leave this girl alone was enough to get me to my feet.

"I want another look at the forest," I added with a grin of my own. "Fey might find something we missed."

"Go," Father said, "and learn what you can."

Agna pushed away from Flo and quickly followed me outside. Once outside, she breathed deeply. "Thank you."

"For what?"

She glanced back at the tent.

"Aye." I nodded. Any girl would be frightened of Flo, even I found him a bit peculiar, though I didn't have to worry about him sneaking a look up my dress.

I whistled and Fey trotted to me. Agna turned and with a dagger in hand, glanced at Fey.

"He's a friend," I said.

"It's not him I'm worried about . . . I no longer trust the forest."

6

ear gripped my heart. Each crush of leaves under our feet or snap of a branch, made me jump. I was afraid of the undead creatures and afraid to bring this boy to Yaya.

"What's your name?" I glanced over at the young Viking. He had no hair on his face and a strong jawline. I wondered if he shaved or was too young to grow a full beard.

"Folkvarr." His deep voice rumbled like the river, too deep for a boy younger than me.

"I'm Agna."

"I know."

My cheeks burned at his callous response, and I cursed my foolishness. Of course he knew my name. I spoke it in front of everyone earlier.

Black markings covered his right hand, disappearing under his shirt. The tip of a black wing peeked out of his collar and spread across his neck, ending just below his ear. His blond hair had two thin braids, one on each side of his face, twined with red fabric, and swung with the breeze, tickling the sides of his cheeks. He had a hard, yet handsome look, and blue-gray eyes that reminded me of the river's mist.

His brows narrowed.

I had stared too long. "Her home is just ahead." My cheeks burned even brighter and I walked faster.

Yaya had always lived in the forest. When Grandfather passed all those years ago, Mama begged her to move into the settlement, but Yaya always answered with: the forest is my home. When our parents were murdered, Yaya took us there, but after many weeks, I decided to return and restore what we had lost. Danica, only thirteen then, was tormented by nightmares and afraid to leave Yaya's side. She stayed while Mama's sister, Aunt Jasna, helped me restore our home.

The trees broke into a clearing. A brook traveled alongside the thatched home and flowers matching the bright colors of the rainbow sprouted from the ground. I stopped, staring at Yaya's house, debating whether or not to bring this stranger inside. The wolf brushed against my side. I looked down at his yellow eyes and wondered if this beast was nudging me forward.

"He only bites if I order him to."

I slowly lifted my hand and the wolf allowed me to pet his head. "He doesn't seem so frightening to me." Fey nudged me once more before dashing off into the woods.

"Are we waiting for something?" Folkvarr asked.

"No." I stepped forward and opened the door.

Fire burned from the hearth at the far wall. A black pot sat on top, filling the room with the familiar onion and garlic scent. Yaya's old rocker sat silent near the hearth, her knit work placed on the red blanket draped over the chair. I peeked inside the pot and saw garlic, onion, parsley and milk-caps boiling in water.

"She must be gathering," I said, knowing she rarely left home for anything else.

"Then we'll wait." Folkvarr removed his shield and sat on the furs lying on the floor.

I picked up Yaya's needlework, admiring the red and white stitch pattern on the kerchief. She had a gift for stitching, one my Aunt Jasna had inherited. Aunt Jasna lived in Kiev. Once a month she journeyed here to visit with us and collect scarves from Yaya to sell in the market.

I had no special skill or talent to call my own. Even Danica had a gift. She had an eye for gathering, and blended herbs into healing tonics of all types.

Folkvarr sat silent, staring at the door as if his gaze would bring Yaya home sooner. He sat stiff and straight as if the warm furs he rested on were a pile of briars.

Tired of the silence, I spoke. "Where are you from?"

"Novgorod, and before that, across the seas. My family traveled here when I was a boy."

"Where's your family now?"

He peeled his gaze from the door to me. "My mother is in Novgorod with my sister and younger brothers. Holmgeirr is my father."

"Holmgeirr?"

"He's the big one."

The giant who sliced Juri down. My eyes watered at the memory of Juri's fate. "Why did he kill him? Juri was a kind man."

"He lied and tried to send us away."

"Is that enough cause for murder?"

"Yes."

My heart raced. "You Northmen care nothing for life."

Folkvarr stood, his mouth in a hard line. I met his glare, but when he shifted closer, I pressed against the back of the chair.

"What do you know of Northmen?" He leaned over me, gazing at me with those piercing eyes.

I gripped the armrests for support. "I know they murdered my parents."

We stared at one another, the silence stretching between us. I waited for him to speak, to argue I was wrong.

"Agna?"

Yaya stood in the doorway holding a basket. I leapt to my feet, brushing Folkvarr aside, and ran into Yaya's arms. She wrapped an arm around my back and I breathed in her clove and honey scent. "I missed you."

She patted my head. "I just saw you yesterday, child."

A tear slipped from my eye. "But so much has happened since then."

I held onto her as she closed the door. "And who is this young man?"

"My name is Folkvarr."

"You may call me Yaya. My true name was lost many years ago."

Wrinkles creased her soft face and her long wavy hair had grayed long ago, but her green eyes sparkled with much life. She never appeared feeble or weak.

"Put these in the pot." Yaya handed me a basket filled with

milk-caps. "I ran out."

I took the white mushrooms and one by one dropped them into the water.

"While Agna attends to the meal, you may tell me what has transpired."

Folkvarr told her everything. I was shocked to hear the details of the undead he had fought. The news startled me so much, I crushed two caps in my hand. He talked about Juri's death as if it was natural and just. Yaya said nothing until the whole tale had been told.

"These are dark times." Yaya waved for me to sit beside her.

I sat on the floor and she held my hand as she spoke.

"The dead do not rise on their own. A witch has summoned them."

"How do we find this witch?" Folkvarr asked.

"You must find the summoning location where she performed the ritual. The earth will be marked—the same mark will be burned into her skin."

"How do you know so much about this?"

I squeezed Yaya's hand, afraid for her to answer his question.

"The leshie told me."

"You knew?"

Yaya turned to me, smiling. "I never trust what they say, but when this Viking spoke, he said truth. Then I knew the wood spirits had been truthful in their words."

Folkvarr grabbed his shield. "Do you know where this summon spot is?"

"No, but the willow will tell you."

"The willow?"

I stood, still holding Yaya's hand. "The oldest spirit of the wood."

Yaya nodded. "Do you remember the way?"

"Yes."

The night our parents died, Yaya led us into the woods. She held our hands and showed us the way to the ancient tree. The one place we would be safe.

"Then go," she said. "Before more of us are lost to this threat."

I hugged Yaya, soaking in her warmth and strength.

"Take Lew with you," she added before letting go.

I sighed. "Yaya, how is an old ram going to help us?"

"He will protect you."

I glanced at the axes hanging from Folkavarr's belt. "We will be fine."

"He goes."

There was no arguing with Yaya when her mind had been set. "Fine, but if he starts nibbling on my rubaKHa I'm sending him home."

Folkvarr arched an eyebrow at my words and I rolled my eyes. "Let's leave."

We walked to the back of the house where Lew chewed on the grass. I unhooked the latch to his gate.

"Is that a sheep?" Folkvarr asked.

"Yes." I placed a hand on my hip, frowning at the animal as he ignored my presence and continued eating. "Yaya says you're to come with us."

Lew stopped chewing and puffed at the air.

"I don't want you to come either." I pointed at the gate.

"But Yaya says it. Out."

Folkvarr's mouth hung open at the sight of Lew barely squeezing through his gate. Three hundred pounds of brown stubbornness. The ram did have one or more uses. His horns were treacherous. They curled forward, the tips facing out, ready to pierce anyone who annoyed him. His head passed my waist, in perfect nibbling distance of my apron. I moved aside.

"Are we really taking him with us?"

As the words left his lips, Fey jumped out from behind a tree, flying through the air at Lew. Lew rammed his head to the side, throwing Fey off in one simple swoop.

Folkvarr laughed.

"Lew!" I yelled, "*Otstan' uzhe!*"

Fey rolled to his feet and shook his head.

"He's fine. Not accustomed to being rammed. Our sheep aren't nearly as fierce." Folkvarr laughed again and smiled, revealing the slightest dimple in his cheek.

He wasn't nearly as terrifying when he laughed. Though, I would never forget what *his* people did. I had to remember, he was still my enemy.

7

The brook weaved through the dense wood, sometimes disappearing through the brush and reappearing a few trees later. Large pines crowded around thick forest, leaving acorns and needles that crushed under our feet. The further we walked, the more I wondered if the undead would cross our path. I had no desire to see those cursed men again.

"What's the willow?" I asked. Slavic culture contained different gods and spirits. I'd never heard of the willow before today, and I needed to understand what awaited me.

"In the heart of our woods lives an ancient tree. The tales say it's the oldest living thing here, planted by Perun himself. There." Agna pointed through the slip of trees where the brook ran. "Do you see it?" Light touched her face, brightening the green in her eyes to the color of fresh moss.

The brook ran into a wide clearing and split around the biggest tree I'd set my eyes on. Its leaves brushed across the flowing grass in wide strides. Pale pink petals dotted the trees and puffs of white floated in the air around it.

Agna put a hand on my chest, stopping me from entering. "This is my people's most sacred place."

I saw the hidden meaning in her cold gaze. "We won't stay long."

She nodded, then turned and took slow steps to the old tree, holding her hands against her chest.

The air tingled and I sensed the presence of the gods.

"Sacred Willow." Agna approached the tree. White puffs surrounded her, whipping in circles like a wild wind. "We seek your guidance. There are unnatural creatures in this land and we seek the place that created them."

A breeze whooshed around the tree and long branches reached toward Agna.

I grabbed my axes but stopped at Agna's raised hand. With her back still facing me, I wondered if she was frightened of the living tree.

"Will you help us?" Her voice carried on the wind. Petals broke away from the tree and swirled in the air and the strange white puffs shot out to the right, leaving the glade. She spun around with a big smile and her face glowed. "Come on!"

And she ran.

"Agna!"

Fey and Lew chased after her. I kept the three of them in my sights while checking our rear. We ran deeper into the forest, further away from the willow. The sunlight began to fade and the thick pine trees changed to mangy oaks. Rot tainted the air, filling my nostrils with the acrid stench of death.

Lew stopped short and Agna crashed into the ram. "*Oh, blin!*"

White puffs whirred in the air around a flattened area of

brush. I walked closer trying to discern what the puffs were. I snapped out my hands and caught one. Slowly, I opened my hands. On my palm sat a tiny human-like creature, snow white with an impish face, solid black eyes, two holes where a nose should be and four transparent wings that fluttered.

"It's a Will-O-Wisp. Guardians of the willow." Agna leaned over and the Will-O-Wisp flew into the air. "We're here."

No grass grew in this wood full of rotted logs, large mushrooms, and plants that stunk of decaying meat. I grabbed my axes. "What kind of mark are we looking for?"

"I'm not sure. Just look—" Agna gasped.

"What is it?"

She knelt and pushed away dead leaves. Each clear spot revealed earth stained with blood. She moved around me, crawling on her knees, pushing more leaves away until we were in the middle of a large circle with crisscrossing lines.

Agna stood and followed me outside of the strange circle.

We stared at the diagram. A seven pointed star filled the center of the circle and different shaped lines surrounded it. I had seen the lines before on our journeys, they were words, more complex than the runes I was used to seeing.

A shadow casted over us as the clouds blocked the waning sun.

"Now we know what to look for," I said while scanning the forest. "We need to leave."

Agna nodded. "We won't reach Yaya's before nightfall." She looked at me with worried eyes. "I don't want to stay in the woods when it's night. We're not too far from the willow, if we run, we can reach it in time."

"How will a tree protect us?"

A Will-O-Wisp landed on Agna's shoulder. "It is more than just a tree. I'm going. Follow me or run back alone."

Was she testing me? Slav or not. I wasn't going to leave a girl alone in the woods with monsters. "Let's go then."

We charged back through the woods, the wisps flying beside and in front of us. Did they sense the danger night brought? The woods carried a strange sense to it as though it watched us, waiting for the moment we dropped our guard.

Upon entering the sacred glade, Agna went to the brook and drank before splashing her face with water. "I wish we had something to eat."

It was too dark to hunt and I'd left without food, thinking we would've been back before nightfall. The willow bore no fruit, but at the edge of the grass I spotted a bush with red berries on it. I walked and picked one off and smelled it.

"There are wolfberries here," I said, picking a few more.

Agna jumped and ran to me, then started picking at the bush. When her hand was full, she took off her scarf. Her blonde locks fell against her shoulders in long waves. She tied the scarf into a pouch and began to drop berries in it.

I wondered why she covered so much of herself. She wasn't ugly and there was nothing wrong with her hair. Yet, most Slavic girls and women I had seen covered their heads with handkerchiefs and I couldn't understand why. It seemed a nuisance. No shield maiden would ever bother with covering her hair in cloth.

"Why do you wear that around your head?" I asked, pointing to the scarf.

"Oh, the kerchief?" She glanced at the linen now full of berries. "We cover our hair once we marry."

"Where's your husband?"

Her cheeks reddened. "He's . . ." She stalled, her eyes going wide.

"Are you all right?"

"Yes." She cleared her throat and turned her head away from me. "I have no husband, nor does Danica. After our parents were killed, Yaya insisted we wear these, to protect ourselves. Everyone in the settlement knows the truth, but they would never go against Yaya's orders." She shoved a berry in her mouth, ending the conversation.

I gathered a few more from the bush. "Let's sit away from the wood."

Agna gazed into the dark forest and nodded.

Moonlight broke through the treetops, bathing the groove in light. Agna sat on the ground, holding out her hand for a Will-O-Wisp. "Yaya took my sister and me here once. I'll never forget it. It's just as magical now as it was then."

Within the sanctuary of the great tree, a strange calmness hummed through the air. "There's something sacred about this place. I can't deny that."

"Now that we know what the mark looks like. How will we search people? What if the witch isn't here?"

"We'll have a mandatory search," I said. "Have them strip down. You can check the women and we'll check the men."

She shook her head. "I just can't believe one of our own could perform something so dark. We're good people."

"People do strange things for even stranger reasons. Juri

must've known. We'll start with his servants."

Hsssssss.

The sound came from the woods.

Agna's face paled. "Folkvarr . . ."

I held a hand out to quiet her and slowly stood, taking an axe in each hand.

Hsssss.

Fey growled beside me, and the old ram shoved himself in front of Agna.

I searched the darkness until I saw a pair of eyes glowing in the dark.

"Don't." Agna grabbed my cape as she stood behind me. "It could be *them.*"

Hssss.

This time the noise came from our left. I turned and saw another set of eyes. Agna held on tighter as an undead man walked forward, revealing its pale, rotted face in the moonlight. When it stuck its foot onto the grass, it moved no more. I looked ahead of us and saw three others do the same. All three struggled and hissed against their frozen legs.

"What do we do? There's too many." Agna's voice cracked.

I reached behind me and pushed her closer to the tree, keeping myself and the animals surrounding her.

One by one, the undead came out of the shadows, circling the entire grove. My heart raced at the sight of them all. Some had flesh falling off their cheeks, while others seemed almost alive—pale, strange red eyes, but mostly intact. What were these creatures?

A stone smacked my face. I swirled around to the left, axes

ready. One of the undead held a rock in his hand, grinning. Blood trickled down the corner of its mouth. I met its red gaze, searching for awareness.

He vaulted another rock, and I ducked.

"Stay here," I said, lifting my axes.

"No!" Agna grabbed my arm. The fear in her voice reflected my own, but I had to know if these monsters could enter the glade.

I grabbed her shaking hand. "Don't be afraid. Stay," I ordered Fey.

Agna cowered behind Fey and Lew, both animals creating a barrier of protection. If I fell, those two would give the undead one hell of a fight, giving her a chance to escape.

With my axes drawn, I walked to the creature who threw the rock. Dirt covered its blotchy face, but its eyes seemed clear and awake. It hovered at the edge. I walked until I was an arm's length away then swung my axe forward. It jumped back, dodging the attack, keeping its sickly gaze on me.

"Come out . . . cooome . . . oouuuttt," it slurred, in a failed attempt to lure me away from the grove.

In a swift move, I grabbed the small knife on my belt and threw it into the creature's face. It landed between the eyes with a sickening thud. The smile disappeared as the undead fell back into the brush.

What are these things?

Running off by myself with Agna wasn't smart. Fighting all these monsters by myself would take an act of the gods. I walked around the clearing, swinging my axes at each creature to see if they would enter the glade. All were the same, frozen on the edge of the grass until I swung and they retreated, but only for a moment. Satisfied they would not enter the glade, I went back to Agna.

"They won't come in here," I assured her. "When morning comes, hopefully they'll return home." Taking her arm, I guided her closer to the tree. "We'll sleep next to the tree. We'll be safe."

"I can't sleep with them so close." She lowered to the ground, her arms shaking. "What do they want? Why are they here?"

I took off my shield and leaned against the tree. Agna slid closer to Lew who laid on the ground. She wrapped her arms around herself, staring wide-eyed at the undead hissing at the edges of the glade.

"The glade protects us." I had to believe they wouldn't enter. There were too many for me to fight by myself. Even with Fey, the most we could handle might be five. Could Agna fight? Maybe against a normal man or beast, but something made from a nightmare? I could barely hold the fear back myself.

She looked at me, her eyes wide. "Don't let them get near us."

"I won't." And I meant it. Whether Slav or Viking, no one deserved a fate met by those creatures. If it came to blows, I would fight until my legs could no longer hold me.

8

The sweet sound of chirping shook me from slumber. Bright sunlight touched the forest floor and warmed my face. I rubbed my eyes, glancing around at the quiet glade. Folkvarr slept against the tree, an axe in each hand. His chest rose with deep breaths and I wondered when he'd slept last. My apron tugged as Lew nibbled away at the fabric.

I ripped my apron from his mouth. "Shoo!" I tried keeping my voice hushed, but Folkvarr stirred.

His eyes opened, squinting at the forest light.

"Good morning," I said.

He looked around, confused at first. "Morning." He rubbed his face. "How long have you been awake?"

"Not long. Lew only managed to eat a sliver of my apron."

Folkvarr gazed at the hole and smiled. "Is he part goat?"

"Who knows? He only eats *my* clothes."

At that, Folkvarr laughed and the sound made my chest flutter. Why did this stranger cause me to feel such a range of emotions: anger, hurt . . . excitement? We had survived the night, together. Folkvarr made me feel safe, something a Viking has never done. It's always been fear and rage around the Northmen.

Could he really be different?

Folkvarr stood, grabbing his shield and placing it on his back. "We should leave. My father will be wondering why I haven't returned."

"Do you think it's safe?" I brushed the grass from my dress, following his lead, and nudged Lew's massive head aside. "What if those things are still out there?"

"Do you know how to fight?"

I averted my gaze from his, thinking of all the times I thought about grabbing my father's old sword and taking revenge. "I've never had to."

"Take this." Folkvarr held out a long dagger, the handle made from bone, though I couldn't discern whether it came from an animal or human remains.

"I have my own knife." I slid a much smaller dagger out of my apron and showed it to him.

His lip curled upward into a smirk. "And what do you use that for?"

"It has lots of uses." I defended my little knife. While it wasn't the length of his, it was sharp and could cut skin like any other blade.

Folkvarr grabbed my wrist and pointed the knife at his chest. He stood inches away, two heads taller than me. "This is how close you'll need to be to do enough damage to kill."

My face burned from his intense gaze. Tiny freckles dotted

his nose and cheeks, so light I would've never noticed unless we were this close and standing in sunlight. My senses seemed to come alive at the touch of his rough hands. The birds sounded louder, morning dew tickled my nose, and the world shined brighter as if the sun sent her rays only on us.

No, this was wrong.

Hiding the strange flutters stirring in my stomach, I pulled my hand away. "I'll be fine. Lew," I called, eager to get back home. "Time to go back to Yaya's."

Folkvarr watched me for a moment. His brow narrowed, and when our gazes met, he held mine for a moment, forcing me to stare into his stormy blue eyes. "Are you all right?" he asked.

"Yes, why?"

"Your cheeks are red."

I spun around, embarrassed. "It's warm."

A lie and one I knew he wouldn't believe for the air had a morning chill. While I would try and hide my thoughts, my body betrayed me. I walked forward, not wanting to turn around and see his expression. I was acting like a foolish girl, and Yaya taught me better.

While Danica had kissed a boy, I had never, not because I didn't want to or didn't think about it, but I couldn't focus on boys when I had to take care of my sister. Marrying would mean leaving her, and I wasn't ready to do that.

Aunt Jasna constantly reminded us both of how we were of age, and two perfectly-beautiful girls should be wed. Yaya never forced either of us. I didn't think she wanted us away from her. Aunt Jasna had warned Yaya we would not be able to pretend to be married much longer. The settlement obeyed

Yaya, but once she passed, our protection would be gone.

Taking a deep breath, I reminded myself why I was out here, and led the way back to Yaya's. Folkvarr and his gray wolf walked alongside Lew and I. Folkvarr said little, but he held his axes ready, his gaze darting around at the trees. Fear slicked the back of my neck, yet, somehow I knew the undead would not come out in this bright light.

When we reached Yaya's, I put Lew in his pen and went inside to say a quick goodbye. Folkvarr waited, even though I said I could make the rest of the journey home by myself.

Yaya sat in her rocker, knitting. "Did you find it?"

I nodded. "Yes."

She placed the knitting down and I sat by her side. "I don't understand any of this. Who would do this?"

She stroked my cheek. "It will be all right. I may not approve of the Northmen, but I know they won't allow such creatures to live. Once this threat is dealt with they'll return home and things will go back to how they were."

Which meant Folkvarr would leave as well.

"Ah," she said.

"What is it?"

Yaya smiled and sat back in her rocker. "Would you like them to stay, perhaps just one of them?"

I stood and folded my arms. "Don't be silly."

"It's okay, child. He's not like the others, but be warned. Our people would never accept a Northmen."

"You speak as if I were to marry? He's a stranger and a Viking."

She rocked back and forth, picking up her needlework. "Be careful my dear, the voldak are not an easy foe, and one I have never encountered. Let us pray to Perun they find the witch or warlock quickly."

A shudder ran through me. Voldak. Papa had shared old tales of the undead men. Stories passed on by his grandfather. If I had not seen them with my own eyes, I would not believe any of this to be real.

Men who lived off the blood of the living.

Men who should be in their graves.

Men who went against the natural law and lived when they should not.

I gave Yaya a quick kiss then rushed out of the house. The quicker we found the witch, the faster the voldak would be gone.

Folkvarr stood outside swinging his axes in vicious arcs. I watched him whirl them around his body, dancing with them.

He noticed me and stopped. "Ready?"

"Yes."

Our voyage home was quiet and uneventful. Neither of us spoke and the silence fell heavy around us. When he reached the settlement, I turned to go home.

"Where are you going?" Folkvarr asked.

"Home?"

"We need to inform my father of what we've learned." He pointed to the longhouse at the top of the hill.

I wanted to cry. My body ached, my head hurt, and I had to let my sister know I was okay.

"I'll make sure you can visit your sister soon," he said softer as if reading my very thoughts.

I held in the frustration, knowing screaming would get me nowhere. He couldn't order me around, but his father had taken over the leadership. There was no defying it, but Folkvarr's words showed his understanding.

Maybe he was different.

9

When I returned, I told my father everything Yaya had spoken, what transpired at the old tree, and our plan to ferret out the witch.

Vega paced behind him. "Dark magic. These Slavs care nothing for honor."

Father stood. "We start now." And he walked outside.

Flo grabbed a horn on his way out and we filed around my father who stood on the hill, overlooking the settlement. Flo blew the horn, holding the note then blew again and again until every villager gathered near.

"A witch hides among you," Father shouted to the crowd. "Everyone will line up and you will be searched. No one is allowed to leave until I say our task is complete."

"You and Flo," Father said, pointing at Vega, "watch the borders. I'll stand guard while Folkvarr searchers for the mark."

Danica appeared out of the crowd, searching for Agna. I nodded my head toward the longhouse and Agna tugged her sister toward me.

"Danica is going to help me," Agna said to me.

"Make sure you check her first."

"What?" Agna's mouth dropped open. "How could you ask such a thing?"

I closed the gap between us, meeting her stubborn gaze. "Everyone gets searched."

"It's okay, Agna," Danica said as she tugged Agna's arm. "Search me then I'll help with the rest."

Agna frowned at me. I waited for her to argue, but she didn't. "Very well. Can the women be searched privately?"

"Yes. Take the back of the room, behind the furs. Fey will stand guard." I whistled, and Fey trotted to my side. "Go with them."

Fey brushed against Agna's side and she scratched behind his ear. It seemed my oldest friend had a soft spot for the blonde.

"I'll start sending them in." Agna spun around, almost dragging her sister alongside her. What did she have to be angry about? Her own flesh told her what we must do. Sister or not, no one was safe.

My father called the men one by one and had them strip. Every torso, arm, hand and leg was clean. No marks. Someone cast that spell, but if not this settlement, then where and why?

By the time the sun had fallen, I had seen more naked men than I cared for.

"There's nothing," I said when Father let the last man go.

"Do you trust this girl?" Father folded his arms while he watched the Slavs return to their homes. The lines on his forehead crinkled. I wondered what he could be thinking.

"She's loyal to her people, but I know she fears the undead. I'll keep watch on her."

Father nodded. "We cannot trust these people. While we bring trade and opportunity, they play in the dirt telling witch's tales and cursing our presence. Though they show fealty to Rurik, they'd prefer to see us all dead." He turned his head on the last word, watching Agna and Danica approach us. I could see the hate and distrust swirling around in his eyes. He had lost men on our journey from Novgorod to Kiev—men killed by Slavs.

"I didn't find anything," Agna said. "Could it be another settlement?" Her shoulders sagged and she seemed disappointed.

"There's a small settlement near the Dnieper River," Danica added. "No more than a few families."

"Yes, I know the place," Agna replied. "They keep to themselves. We could ask."

Not once did she meet my father's gaze. Could she sense the animosity? I wanted to assure her while my father didn't trust her, I did. She feared the undead more than us, and that's why I knew she would do everything to help us find the source.

"You will take us there tomorrow," Father said. "We leave at dawn."

Agna's mouth opened then shut.

My father wasn't one to ask. Everything he spoke was a statement or a command. I learned long ago, that arguing with him ended with a rap on the head.

With her head bowed she said, "May I return home? It's been a very long two days and I need to rest."

Her sister glared at my father, waiting for his reply. Her cheek twitched, and her narrowed gaze reminded me of what Father said earlier. No, they didn't trust or like us at all.

"Go."

Agna lifted her head and let out a soft sigh. "Thank you."

Our gazes met. She opened her mouth as if to speak, but then bit her bottom lip instead. Danica grabbed Agna's hand, pulling her away before I could say a goodbye.

When Agna turned back to look at me, I wanted to follow her, if only to make sure she returned home safely. Spending the night with her, surrounded by the undead, had awakened this deep desire to protect her.

Father pushed me forward, breaking my contact with Agna. "Don't get any idea about that one."

I spun around. "I don't have any ideas."

The stern face said enough about what my father thought, but he didn't know Agna. She wasn't out to hurt us. She risked her life just like we did.

"You are my son. I see how you watch her."

Puffing out my chest, I met Father's disapproving glance. He was taller, broader, stronger than any Viking I knew, but that didn't make him right about this.

"She's just a girl," I scoffed, holding my ground, pretending not to care. If I showed any emotional attachment, I wasn't sure what he would do with her.

Father took two steps forward, leaning over me. "Remember your place. We trade with the Slavs, nothing more."

"Is that what you were doing the other night? *Trading*?"

He snapped out his wrist, quicker than I expected, and

yanked the front of my shirt. I stumbled forward.

"You have a duty to our people." His voice deepened. "When the undead are dealt with, we return to Novgorod where your brothers are. Do you mean to leave them for a Slav who would kill you the moment your back is turned?"

So many words spun around my mind. Yet, I said nothing, knowing the wrong word would put Agna in danger.

Father let go, and folded his arms. His presence made me want to crawl into a hole. "If she becomes a block in your path. I will remove her."

My chest heaved and an image of Agna's head rolling down the hill passed through my mind. Father wouldn't think twice of killing her.

"She's just a girl," I mumbled.

"Go rest," he ordered. "I'll take first watch." He pushed past me, and I wondered if he was going to spy on Agna or really take first watch.

10

I lay on the cot, desperate for sleep, turning in every direction, but one that was comfortable. The thin blanket itched my skin, and my mind whirled with questions. We had spent the entire day searching for a witch, and found nothing. If the witch wasn't here, where was she? And why would she be raising the dead?

"Have you eaten today?" Danica knelt in front of the oven.

"No." My stomach rolled with uncertainty, fear, and confusion. Every man and woman had been searched and we found nothing. Not a mark.

Food hadn't entered my thoughts once.

"You should eat," Danica said. "There's some rye pie from this morning."

I nodded, rolling to my side and curling into a ball, thinking of the scary stories Papa would tell us about the voldak. He always ended a tale with a shout, which made Danica and me scream like mad. Only once did we hear of a true voldak roaming the lands, but not near Kiev. Papa said not to worry;

it was probably the leshie playing tricks on the local villagers.

Thinking back, I wondered if Papa knew the truth, and kept us innocent with his lies.

Danica brought over a bowl and sat in the chair next to the bed. "Here."

"Thank you." I took the bowl and broke off a piece of the pie. Onion mixed with rye in soft dough that warmed my stomach.

"I have a few wolfberries I can make into a spread," she added.

"You went into the forest?" The closest berry bushes were near the well. The same well the voldak attacked me.

"Only for a short time and it was day."

The few bites began to sour in my stomach. "You *can't* go in there. It's not safe."

Danica's gaze drifted from me to the door. "I can't hide indoors and be afraid."

I placed a hand on her knee. "You have to be careful. These creatures will kill us."

"No."

"No? One attacked me, and last night only the willow protected us from them."

She shook her head and left the chair. "Don't you think it odd these "creatures" show up just as the Vikings did?"

The Vikings had come here because of the rumors.

She paced across the floor. "And don't you think it even odder that they came here claiming undead walk, creatures we have never seen, then kill Juri and take over our home?"

Her words echoed through my mind.

"They brought them. Another excuse to kill us or worse." She spat out the last words as if the mere thought of it revolted inside her.

"I . . . I . . ." Was it possible? Yes. Have Vikings always killed and lied to us? Yes.

Most Vikings stayed north of Kiev, further up the Dnieper River near Novgorod, but with Kiev changing into a hub of trade, each season more of the Northmen traveled here, and not all were kind.

But Yaya said Folkvarr was different. I'd watched the fear in his stormy eyes when the voldak hissed around us. If Vikings were the cause of the dead rising, Folkvarr and the men he traveled with weren't a part of it.

"Don't trust them."

I snapped my head up at Danica's beautifully-paled face.

"I don't—"

"Don't bother lying to me." She turned and grabbed a basket off the shelf. "I won't let them hurt you, even if you're too blind to see the truth."

She shoved open the door and left without another word. I wanted to call after her and argue she knew nothing about the voldak or the Vikings. *We* knew nothing about them. Folkvarr had been kind and showed no signs that any of this was some ruse to enslave our people.

"She doesn't understand," I said aloud, talking to Grandfather as if he were sitting beside me, though the house sat in silence. "It'll be fine. Tomorrow, we'll have better luck."

Hopeful words. Empty words. For I knew darkness hovered over us and the woods. I didn't want to believe Danica's claims, but what did I know? What did any of us know?

The bowl shook in my hands.

Whether the Northmen were behind the voldak or not, didn't matter. The undead owed allegiance to no one. I would die before any of these monsters touched my family. Glancing at the door, I knew Danica was right, the Vikings couldn't be trusted.

But trust was no longer a concern when undead walked the lands.

Folkvarr would fight them, I could trust in that.

11

The northern settlement held nothing but a few shabby homes and goats. Two children with dirty faces sat by a log, playing with a mangy-haired dog. As we approached, an older man came out of the first house, axe in hand.

"We mean you no harm." Agna stepped in front of my father, attempting to hide his imposing form. "We just have some questions."

The man nodded, but his gaze stayed on my father.

"We have had some trouble these past few days," Agna said. "More than just spirits, dead risen from their graves."

The two children looked at the old man and immediately ran inside one of the homes pulling the dog along with them.

"They come at night," the man replied, lowering the axe, though he didn't drop it. "Scratching on our doors, tormenting us. We board everything at night, even brought the goats inside."

"A witch cast the spell to bring them here," I said. "Have you seen anyone strange around these parts?"

He shook his head. "No. You're the first to come here in weeks."

"A dead end," I sighed.

"Maybe not." My father stepped around Agna. "The undead go somewhere during the day. In your encounters, have you seen what direction they come or go?"

"Only once," the man said quietly. "The first sighting was at night. They came from the east."

"The river." I looked east.

"Thank you." Agna bowed her head and turned to leave.

"We'll follow the path to the river and look for clues." Father took lead and we followed.

This day brought the first clear sky since reaching Agna's settlement; even the strange mist seemed to be held at bay. With the sun high, its fiery gaze heated my neck and face. The river rushed and bubbled alongside the pebbled grounds. Quiet and peaceful.

Not long into our journey, Agna asked, "May we stop?" She nibbled her bottom lip and coyly looked away from us. "I need a few moments, alone."

"Go, but not far," Father said.

She nodded then briskly headed to the woods. Her dress swayed with her fast steps, eventually disappearing. *Can't she relieve herself behind a closer bush?*

"Eyes ahead," Father said.

"These are cursed lands," I replied, changing the subject before he could remind me of my "duty." "Never would undead walk on our grounds." I turned away from the woods to face the river.

"Aye, but who are we to judge the gods? Magic runs thick in these parts. Do you not—"

A song drifted to us, soft, warm, inviting. Squinting past the harsh sunlight, I followed the music, Father in step beside me. The river curved around the woods, and there, sitting on a cluster of large rocks by the edge, sat a maiden—so fair and beautiful it had to be Freya come down to visit us. The maiden brushed her long, golden tresses that cascaded in waves across her bare shoulders. Her white dress sparkled beneath the sun, glittering like a pearl picked from the sea. She smiled through her song, gazing upon us with hypnotizing blue eyes.

"Steady," Father whispered, though his voice was lost in the song.

Another maiden appeared beside the first, smiling, and coaxing us closer with her slender fingers. The girls sat like two golden pearls, glowing with an inner brilliance.

"Hello, kind sirs," the first said. "Is it not a beautiful day?"

"Aye," I replied, unable to look away from her. Her skin glimmered with a luminescent glow. I wanted to caress it, to feel the warmth I knew must radiate from within.

Father reached them before I did. I grumbled at the audacity as the second maiden sang her sweet song to him. Lightness filled my head, and longing pulled me forward. I couldn't turn away from the deep blue of the maiden's gaze, or the sparkle glimmering from her outstretched hand.

"Help me," she sang, and I would. I would help her in anything. Kill a hundred men, slay a thousand beasts, whatever it took to ease the sadness her voice carried.

She stretched out her arms. I moved closer, almost to her. Did the undead frighten her? Wind carried her hair in a whirlwind of beauty and my chest ached to touch it.

"Folkvarr!" Agna's voice echoed behind me.

The maidens smiled as one. "Sit with us," they said in unison. One of them had already curled herself against my father.

A thunderous crack hit the back of my head, sending a shot of pain through my skull. I whirled around in a growl.

Agna held another rock in her hand, eyes wide. "Come away!"

"Why did you do that?" I stomped to her, fury filling my steps.

"Don't leave," the maiden sang behind me. "I'm cold, help me."

I turned, ignoring Agna and her strange outburst. Suddenly, something slammed into my back, pushing me face first into the dirt.

"Don't!" Agna cried from on top of me. She wrapped her arms around my neck in a pitiful attempt to keep me grounded.

"What the devil? Get off!" I pushed up, lifting Agna who still held on tightly.

She cupped her hands against my ears. I barely heard her scream my father's name.

A third woman rose out of the river while the two by the rocks reached for my father's arms. He had just enough time to look back at us before they yanked him into the rushing river.

"No!" I shook Agna off me and jumped to my feet. With my axes free, I ran forward, my head suddenly clear.

"Folkvarr!" Agna charged in front of me, stopping me with her hands. "You can't."

"Move!" I shoved her aside.

She ran around me, blocking me again, stubborn like her

ram. "He's gone and we must leave!" She held the front of my shirt, refusing to let me pass.

"Leave? Three witches just pulled my father into the river. He needs my help!"

She pressed against my chest, meeting my gaze. "He has been taken by the rusalki."

Fury deeper than the lowest level of Hel coursed through me. "Then show me where to find them."

"Until now, I thought they were only tales." She glanced back at the river as if she expected those creatures to slither back out.

"What are they?"

"Water spirits." She stepped back dropping her hands to cover her mouth.

"This land is cursed." I spat. "I will find my own way to my father."

"This all started with those undead. The spirits are acting out." She shook her head. "Every story I've been told as a child has become real. I've always known the lands to hold magic and mystery, but to see them with my own eyes . . ."

I whistled and Fey darted out from the woods. I watched the water expecting Father to crawl onto the bank, his broadsword in one hand, a rusalka head in the other, but he didn't. The water roared in the river, tumbling north and south.

I slid my axes back into my belt and turned toward the village.

They would pay.

They would all pay.

12

What do you say to the boy who just watched his Father disappear? I had no words of comfort nor wisdom to share. With both my parents gone, I understood the hopelessness of absence—the ache left from the separation of someone you hold dear.

Folkvarr stormed through the brush like a wild boar. Holding my rubaKHa, I ran after him, but at his fast pace, I fell behind. Panic rose in my chest. What would happen when he reached the village? Would his anger lash out at our home? Would his companions kill us all? Or would they do what all Vikings do: rape, murder, destroy.

I slammed my feet against the ground as I ran faster than I ever had, my breath hitching in my throat and burning my chest. No matter what vengeance Folkvarr sought, I wouldn't let him hurt anyone.

I caught up to him just as he reached the village.

"Vega! Flo!" Folkvarr's yell blasted out, causing heads to

turn. "Vega!" he screamed again, running around, turning his head, trying to look everywhere at once.

"I'm here." Vega appeared from the left where the blacksmith wheel was. He glanced at Folkvarr then at me. "Where's Holmgeirr?"

Folkvarr's jaw twitched and his knuckles whitened as he gripped his axes. "Gone."

"Gone?" Vega's face hardened. "Tell me what happened."

"Three witches pulled him into the river." Folkvarr paced. "They did something to us."

"Rusalki," I added. "Water spirits who seek out men and take them under the water to their palace, for all time."

"You saw one?" Danica's eyes widened in excitement as she darted to my side. "Are they just like the stories?"

Her slight burst of excitement stopped at the low growl coming from Folkvarr. "If you are so excited then you will help us find them."

Danica backed away from him. "I didn't mean to offend."

"Yet you did," he snapped back.

"Arguing is only wasting time." Vega grabbed the back of Folkvarr's hood and pulled him away from Danica. "Where can we find this place?"

Danica and I looked at each other. Her eyes pleaded with mine, but the stories never spoke of where they lived. "I . . . I don't know."

Folkvarr's jaw twitched. The anger rolled off him in a wave, and my heart tightened, not out of fear, but out of understanding. "But Yaya will know," I added. "She will know something."

"I will stay and wait for Flo to return," Vega said. "Return once you know where. We still have the undead to deal with." Vega slapped a hand on Folkvarr's shoulder.

"Aye," Folkvarr huffed and charged off in the direction of Yaya's.

"I'll come with you," Danica whispered to me. "You mustn't bear this alone."

"No," I said. "Stay here." I grabbed her hands. "Don't worry, sister. We'll return soon. Someone needs to keep watch over the village."

"Be back before night." She squeezed my hand before letting go.

"I will." I hugged her and kissed her cheek.

Folkvarr and Fey dashed through the forest, forcing me to run until my chest begged for air. "Will you wait?" I called after him, though he showed no signs of slowing.

"Run faster," he shouted.

Otstan' uzhe. "I *am* running faster!"

Folkvarr stopped. Thankfully, he couldn't see the glistening sweat on my face. I slowed, reaching him, and rested my hands on my thighs to catch my breath.

"Just a moment," I huffed, and wiped my forehead with the back of my hand. "We're almost there. No need to run anymore."

Folkvarr stood silent and brooding, staring off into the winds. Was he angry at me for what happened? When I saw the maidens seducing them, I knew I only had a chance at saving Folkvarr.

He turned, catching me staring.

"I think I hear Yaya." I ignored his questioning expression and dashed ahead.

"There she is." Folkvarr pointed at Lew's pen. Yaya stood outside with a bucket on her hip, tossing old apples over the fence.

"Yaya!" She smiled at my voice, and I waved.

"Returned so soon?" She wrapped an arm around me as I hugged her.

"Yes. We need help."

She grinned at Folkvarr. "I see your friend has returned as well. Good day, Folkvarr."

"Good day," he said with a nod. I was surprised he replied at all. Seemed even when he was upset, he still had manners.

"Yaya, we must speak, inside." I tugged her away from Lew, whispering as if the maidens could hear me from here.

"Very well, child."

Sage hung in bunches above the entryway and more littered the hut. If Yaya thought she needed sage to cleanse the home, things were most certainly not well.

She picked up her knitting and sat in her rocker. Folkvarr stood, rigid like an oak. I sat among the furs.

"Something has happened," Yaya said. The rocker creaked as she swayed back and forth in it.

"Yes." I glanced at Folkvarr, wondering if he wanted to speak or if I should. When he said nothing, I continued. "Folkvarr's father was taken by the rusalki."

Yaya stopped rocking and dropped the knitting in her lap. "Rusal'naya is not for another month. They should not be ashore."

Once a year the water maidens would leave their abode during the weeklong festival, where we celebrated and performed the rites to dispatch unclean spirits. Though no one ever saw the rusalki, stories of men vanishing, shortly followed. After the festival, the maidens were confined to the river where they would reside until the following year.

I can't believe the stories are all true. Looking at Yaya, I pleaded with her. "Will you help us?"

She shook her head. "I cannot."

"Can't or won't?" Folkvarr's tone matched the fury crinkling his forehead.

"Can't. But Agna can."

"Me? How?"

"You must speak with the leshie."

"Yaya, you are the only one they've ever spoken to. I have never even seen one." Hopelessness flooded my chest.

"You will summon one."

"Hasn't magic caused us enough?" Folkvarr's face softened as if he worried for my safety.

Our gazes met, and for a moment, kindness and warmth sprinkled out of his eyes. The corner of his lip curled ever so slightly, and in that I understood that we were in this together.

"She will not be harmed," Yaya replied. "But Agna *must* go alone."

"What?" We both spoke and turned to Yaya who had left the rocker and stood before us.

"You are not from our lands. The leshie will not appear if you are present."

"So I am to leave her?" Folkvarr's voice rose. "To the wilds and the undead and witches who drown and kill?"

"Folkvarr." I placed a hand on his arm. While his concern filled me with warmth, I did not want him and Yaya arguing.

"I know you worry, boy," Yaya said. "But Agna belongs to these lands. She is a child of the wood. If she calls upon the woodland spirits, they will come."

"*Vnuchenka.*" Yaya placed a hand on each side of my face, smiling. "You hold greatness in your heart, never fear that. I will show you how to summon a leshii. When one appears, speak truth, and ask for the entrance to the rusalki's palace."

"I'm afraid."

Tears shone in her wise eyes. "That is why Lew will go with you."

"Ugh."

Folkvarr snorted a laughed. I glared at him, and he scratched the side of his face trying to cover his smirk.

13

gna's shoulders slumped as she unhitched the gate for Lew. The old ram squeezed through, butting her hip in the process.

"*Oh blin!*" She smacked Lew on the back of the head, sending him such an icy stare her green eyes shimmered blue.

I scratched the top of Lew's head. He chewed a mouthful of grass which slopped out the side of his mouth. Agna may have no patience for the beast, but I liked him. His gray-white wool needed a good shearing soon.

"Does Yaya cut his coat?" I asked, patting Lew one more time near his massive horns.

"Who cares?" Agna wrinkled her nose. "Can we hurry? I want to be back before night."

She hugged herself and glanced at the sky. Sunlight beamed against her green eyes. I sensed the fear behind them. Not many things scared me, but seeing an undead man walk, shook my bones. Never moving on, aimless in this world, never reaching the splendors of Valhalla. It was the worst fate any man or woman could have.

Our journey to the willow was as somber as Lew's coat. Agna said little, and constantly rung her apron in her hands. I didn't pretend to understand her thoughts, for my own settled on my father. By the gods did I never think anything, or anyone could hurt him. Yet, he fell before my eyes to a trio of golden- haired maidens.

How did he not sense the danger? How did I not?

I remembered how intense desire and longing coursed through me, and sadness. A sadness so great I believed the only way to quench it was to touch the maiden's locks and help them in whatever cause they needed.

I was a damn fool.

If Flo had accompanied us, he would have drowned and never wanted to be found. I would make sure he would stay far away from the rusalki's palace.

"We will find him." Agna's soft voice broke through my thoughts.

"Aye."

We gazed upon one another, longer than we should have. She would risk her life for someone she barely knew and for a people who had stolen too much. I didn't know why she had decided to help, only that I knew she would stay true to her word.

"What?" she said, scrunching her button nose.

"Do you know how to use a sword?"

"Of course." Her gaze flitted to the tall trees, avoiding me.

"You need to know how to fight, if you are going to go out alone."

"I know . . ." Her words trailed off and she turned forward, quickly walking to the willow.

Seeing the sacred tree a second time did nothing to extinguish the ancient aura pulsating in the area. Will-O-Wisps flew around the large branches and us. I raised a hand and one landed on my finger, tilting its tiny head in my direction.

"I should hurry." Agna rubbed her hands against one another.

I placed a hand on her shoulder and she jumped. "Take this." I handed her one of my daggers.

Her hands trembled as she took the weapon from me.

I covered my hands over hers. "Do you trust Yaya?"

"Always," she croaked.

"Then trust in her words. If she says you will be safe, believe her. And I will be waiting here for you."

"What if . . . what if I don't make it back in time? What if I get stuck out there, with *them?*"

I cupped the side of her face. "Then I will come for you." Sadness drenched her perfect eyes. I didn't want her to go.

"Promise?"

"Aye."

14

I had never been so grateful for Lew. The old ram never stopped to eat, or nibble at my dress, even though I was within nibbling distance. He trotted close to my side, quiet. His presence helped move me forward. While I wasn't quite sure how he would help in actual danger, knowing I had a three hundred pound irritable ram with me eased my fears.

Yaya never said how far I needed to be from the willow only that it had to be far enough from Folkvarr, and in a clearing where I could create the summoning circle. I gathered birch branches that scattered the ground, listening for the snaps of unwanted creatures. The trees and wild ferns became more spaced in this area, creating a small clearing. Sunlight broke through the mist, and I thanked Perun for the clear sky. I took a deep breath, and slowly placed the branches in a circle with the tips pointed in. Lew wandered off to the side and chomped on a fern.

"It's time."

With a careful step, I entered the circle. "I call upon the

master of the wood. Kind leshii, hear my plea. I seek your aid in a troubling time. Will you not grant this lowly soul the honor of your presence?"

Wind rattled the trees and blew my hair back. My heart thumped as wild as the spirits. What would the leshii look like? So many stories talked about horned demons, fire burning like coals in their soulless eyes, a voice rough and earth-shattering. They were immense, powerful, and terrifying.

"A girl as pretty as you should not play this deep in the forest."

I whirled around at the honeyed voice.

A shirtless boy leaned against a tree. His relaxed posture matched the easy grin on his face. No horns, no animal like quality. Was this a leshii?

"You're a boy?"

He stepped away from the tree. His body shrunk and sprouted black feathers as he transformed into a bird and flew through the air then just as swiftly shifted back into a boy as he landed in front of me. "Am I?"

I flinched and he laughed.

The stories held some truth—his eyes were the color of burning coals.

He shook out his auburn hair and stretched his arms behind his head. "What do you want, *krasavitza moya?*"

His sweet words would not sway me. Yaya warned me to be careful. "I seek your aid."

Yawning, he waltzed around me. "So you said. In what, though?"

"The rusalki palace."

"Tsk. Tsk." He wagged a finger then bopped my nose with

it. "Not a place for you. Not even I like it there."

"So you know the way? Will you take me?"

He eyed me with curiosity. "Why would you want to go there? You'll most likely die."

I gulped back my fear. If I understood anything about the forest, it was that they did not take kindly to foreigners. "My reasons are my own."

"Ahh," he smiled, tapping his chin. "Your lover has been taken."

Heat flushed my face. "No."

"Hmpf. Haven't consummated the relationship yet?"

I shoved him away. "Watch your tongue, leshii."

His smiled faded, and coldness pricked my skin. "My help comes with a price. Will you pay it?"

Holding my chin high, I met his fiery gaze. "I will."

"Good." His smile returned. "I will take you to the rusalki palace in exchange for one human soul."

"What?"

His lip curled into a devilish grin. "Yours."

I covered my mouth with my hand.

"A simple price to pay for such an elusive secret."

Remembering what Yaya said about the bargain, I pulled the amber stone out of my pocket. "I've brought a bargain price."

He scrunched his forehead and titled his head to the side. "You want to bargain with that?"

"Yes."

Don't show fear. Hold your head high.

A boisterous laugh had him hunched over, slapping his leg. He kept laughing. I didn't know whether to be insulted or mad.

"Do you accept the trade?" I held the stone out in my hand.

"That?" He laughed again, holding his stomach. "Oh, *krasavitza moya*, you know very little of my kind."

No matter how many times he called me his beauty, it did nothing to settle the nerves filling my belly.

The laughing subsided, and he swung his arms behind his back, eyeing me with a wicked grin. "My price for this request would be a thousand amber stones, or one human soul."

An impossible request. No one had that much amber.

Could I hand over my soul for a man I didn't even know? I had no ties to Holmgeirr, and his people had murdered my parents. Still . . .

"What happens if I say yes?"

"I will keep my word. I will show you the hidden palace. After, you will be allowed to go home, but soon I will come for you. You will belong to *me*."

"To do what? Wash the dirt from your feet or the stench from your hair?" My body shook with fear, anger, and the uncertainty of my future.

The leshii pulled a piece of his hair in front of his nose and sniffed it. "Smells fine to me."

"This is hopeless." Why would Yaya send me here? Didn't she know about the price? The gem she gave me to bargain with was useless.

"Fear not, *krasavitza moya*, for you have found one of the nicer leshii. Should any other have been near, your soul would be in much more danger. We don't always bargain when we are summoned. Sometimes, we take."

His term of endearment did nothing to lessen the fear

beating against my chest.

"I will treat you well," he added. "Once you come to live with me, you won't be allowed to go back to the settlement, but I will allow you to visit your Yaya."

"You know Yaya?"

"Everyone knows the old lady. You have her eyes."

What would Yaya say? I couldn't believe she would want me to risk my soul and my life for a Viking. We owed the Northmen nothing.

Folkvarr's anguished expression of watching his father disappear tormented my thoughts. He had a chance to save his father when I had none. How could I return to him with no answers, when they were in reach? Even if I denied this price, Folkvarr would find his own way, and the chances he would survive were low. As a stranger in this land, the forest would not protect him.

It is the right thing to do. Regardless of heritage, he is still a father who should be reunited with his son. When all is done, I will find a way to break this bargain, even if I have to leave these lands alone.

"Your answer?" The leshii leaned over, smelling of cedar and honey.

"Yes. But you will not only show me the way, you will take me there and back, safely."

"Then let's make haste." He held out his hand which I smacked away. He laughed.

"What should I call you?"

"Kole, and you?"

"Agna."

"Get on, Agna." He shook out his wavy hair. His body grew and elongated, muscle stretching over thick bones, until the boy before me was a stunning elk.

I wrapped my arms around his thick neck, staying clear of his large antlers. Locking my hands together, I held tight as he leapt into the forest. We rushed around the trees, branches breaking in our stead, plants crushed by his heavy hooves. Many nights I had seen the elk run across the far fields, admiring their majestic canter. In all my dreams, I never imagined a leshii could be one of those grand creatures.

The stories only told part of the truth.

The sun dipped lower into the sky. I still had time, but we had to hurry. I wouldn't stay in these woods a moment longer than I needed.

Did the leshii fear the undead? They had to know what haunted their woods. If Kole knew, maybe he would help and I wouldn't have to bargain my soul.

"Do you know of the undead?" I asked.

He snorted, whipping his head to the side.

I guess he can't speak when in that form. Realizing our conversation would be one sided, I kept my fearful thoughts and questions to myself.

The woods blurred by in a flash of brown and deep green. He finally slowed when we reached a mass of overgrown ivy hanging down from a stone hill between two immense, twisted oak trees. Kole dipped to the ground and I slid off.

"There's nothing here?" Wild ivy blocked the path before us.

Kole, back in human form, grinned and waved his hand along the ivy. Green vines crawled away from the center, opening like a window into the woods. A dark cave nestled into the rock, large enough to walk into.

"Are we going in there?"

"Yes," he said. "What do you plan to do once we get there?"

"No, I'm not going to the palace. You only need to show me the way, today."

"Tell me why." The hidden fire in his eyes glowed.

I took a step back, grabbing the hilt of the dagger within my apron. "Our agreement was that you would take me. I made no promise to tell you why."

He grabbed my hand and dragged me to the cave entrance.

"You're hurting me!" I twisted my hand, but his iron grip did not break. "Let go of me."

"Stay close and do not speak or the maidens might hear." Kole dropped my hands and snapped his fingers. Torches alongside the rock walls lit.

I followed his steps, watching the shadows for signs of a rusalka. Salt and a sweet smell, I couldn't place, tickled my nose. Light from the torches bounced off the rocky walls casting dancing shadows as we walked through the cave. My heartbeat roared in my ears.

Men had always been the rusalki's object of affection. I wasn't sure what they would do to a girl strolling their domain. Would Kole side with them?

Don't trust the spirits.

Yaya had reminded Danica and me every full moon, when the forest came alive with music and wild laughs, to never to trust the spirits.

"You always say that Yaya, but I want to see them."

We had always been intrigued by the old tales, and would stare out the round window, searching the night for any truth to them. I never believed the silly stories, even the ones about our house spirit, Grandfather. To me, Grandfather was the old rat that scurried into our home when he thought we were sleeping. Curious animals made for curious spirits. Now, I understood Yaya had always been right, and I should have listened closer when she talked about each spirit, and the dangers found with all.

The cave ended at a pool. Mist hovered over the water, circling it like a hungry wind.

Kole pointed.

I knelt by the water, peering closer. Light shone below. A shadow swam near the bottom. Was it a fish or a rusalka? If I looked a little closer . . .

Kole yanked me back, shaking his head, and motioning with it to the entrance of the cave, but I refused and slipped off my shoes. I had to see the palace for myself. I pointed at the pool and mouthed 'take me'.

Grunting, he bowed for me to go first.

I swung my legs into the pool. Warm water splashed against me. I would have thought the temperature would match the frigidness of the river the maidens had appeared from.

Kole coughed and nodded at my clothing.

Right. Swimming in this frock will weigh me down.

Getting to my feet, I grabbed Kole's shoulders and turned him around. Yaya would slay me if she knew I removed my clothing in front of a boy.

But he's not a real boy.

Dusk would soon be upon us, and I would rather shed my dress in front of a pretend boy than face the undead outside. I untied my apron and slid off my rubaKHa and left them against the cave wall. Cold swept through my thin slip, and I turned to the pool below.

I took a giant breath and dove into the water.

Warmth rushed against my skin. With open eyes, I swam deeper, brushing aside the long tendrils of algae hanging from the rocks above. I only needed to swim low enough to see the palace. Shadows swarmed the bottom, slithering around until the entire floor resembled a horde of ants.

Light beamed from the north, and the tall outline of a structure shimmered through the light. The rusalki palace . . . and too far to swim. How could we ever reach the palace? No human could hold their breath that long. Kole touched my shoulder and pointed at the dancing light then back up to the surface. I nodded.

I have my answer.

Glancing down, I noticed a dark writhing mass. Kole followed my gaze, and shrugged before swimming to the bottom.

My lungs tightened and burned. *Hurry Kole*

Kole dove. When he reached the bottom, he flipped around and swiftly swam to me eyes wide. I wondered what had spooked him.

Then the floor rose and hundreds of undead swam toward us.

Kicking my legs, I rushed to the surface, trying not to panic or scream. When I popped out of the water, Kole was by my side, lifting me onto the cave's floor.

"Hurry," he urged, and I raced to grab my clothes.

"They won't follow. The sun hasn't set, yet." I threw my

dress on and re-tied my apron.

Thunder boomed outside and the pounding of heavy rain stomped against the cave. The waning sunlight disappeared behind the clouds.

A pale hand reached out of the pool and grasped the edge.

"Run!" Kole grabbed my hand, dragging me out of the cave.

"The willow!" I screamed over the thunder. "We'll be safe there!"

Branches snagged my legs, scraping them and leaving trails of blood. Briars snatched onto my dress, capturing me. Kole ripped the brush away, but the moans of the undead crept closer. Behind us were twenty, maybe thirty men with pale skin hanging off their bones, hair mangled and knotted, and all of them running.

"We're not going to make it!" My heart leapt with each step, beating wildly.

"Get on." Kole shifted into the elk and I jumped onto his back. A hand lashed out at me and Kole bucked, kicking his legs back and sending the undead away, but another came, this one with a knife.

Kole galloped away from the cave as I held onto his neck.

These undead weren't mindless. When one launched an arrow in our direction, there was no way to stop it. The arrow stabbed into Kole's right flank and he groaned, yet kept running. The creatures chased us with an unnatural speed, suddenly appearing on both sides of us. Another volley, two more hits to Kole. I wanted to rip out the arrow, but the metal tips were the only thing keeping his blood in.

His pace slowed.

Lew charged out of the woods and rammed the nearest voldak. Before another had a chance to slice at his wooly coat, Lew rammed again, his horns gouging the undead in the stomach.

The white top of the willow shone in the gray mist. We were so close!

"Folkvarr!" I screamed as loud as my lungs would let me. "Folkvarr!"

Fey charged past us and at the oncoming horde. Folkvarr's eyes widened at the sight of me and he slid out his axes.

"Keep going," he yelled.

"What about you?"

"I'll cover your rear." His face turned in a hard line and he ran after Fey.

"Almost there, Kole." I rubbed his neck and he moaned. Blood trickled from the arrows stuck in his coat. He barreled through the berry bushes and came to a crashing halt by the tree, falling onto his side.

Quickly, I jumped off and put my hand over the first arrow.

His big black eyes blinked at me.

"Hold on," I said. "I'll remove them."

Placing my hand on the first shaft, I yanked the arrow out. He cried, and I quickly yanked the second one free. His eyes shut and his head lolled to the side. I removed the last arrow, throwing it on the ground. With the arrows removed, Kole shifted back into the shirtless boy. Blood seeped from his wounds and he shivered.

I ripped off my apron and pressed it against the wounds. Clashes, grunts, and Folkvarr's wild scream, echoed through the glade. How he could he fight so many? I wanted to run out and help, but if I removed the pressure against Kole's wounds, the blood loss could kill him.

Wind rushed around the glade, and a loud groan sounded from the giant tree. Roots ripped out of the soil, dragging bits of earth into the air. Branches swayed out of the glade as a powerful wind whooshed with each movement of the ancient tree. With a resonating crash, the willow slammed its branches, shaking the ground. I hovered over Kole, protecting him from the twigs that fell off in the willow's wake.

Again, the willow slammed its long massive limbs back and forth. Leaves splattered the sky and the glade came alive with groans and creaks. I glanced up as a scream blasted the sky. One of the undead was stuck on the willow's branch, and the branch tossed him out to the heaven's, so far, I couldn't see where the undead landed.

My heart squeezed with gratitude as the ancient spirit protected us. Fey howled, and I watched the woods, desperately waiting to see if Folkvarr would return.

Stay alive.

Another scream, and my heart tightened with fear. Was that Folkvarr?

Rain poured around us. I wanted to run out, to see what was happening, but the moment I released pressure on the wounds, blood gushed out.

Where are you?

It seemed wrong to sit here, knowing what Folkvarr faced.

Another creature flew across the sky, and my body shook.

The willow's roots slipped into the dirt and the branches

rested back in their normal position. The groans, yells, and creaks stopped, and I held my breath at the silence.

Where is he? Panic clenched my throat in a silent scream. I was terrified to move. If the undead killed Folkvarr I didn't know what I would do.

A bloody Folkvarr walked back into the glade, Lew and Fey trotting beside him

"By the gods." His eyes were wide as he gazed upon the now sleeping willow. He slid his twin axes back into their holders. "I've never seen anything more magnificent than that tree."

I jumped to my feet, tears streaming my face, and leapt at him.

He caught me, stumbling back a bit.

"You're alive." I dug my face into his neck, gripping him tight.

"Aye. I was almost worried. Those things are hard to kill."

He wrapped his strong arms around my body. I had never felt safer in my life. He killed them. He survived. We both survived.

"It's over," he whispered, turning his face to brush his lips across my cheek. He pressed his hands against my waist, bringing me closer to his chest. "Are you all right?"

I nodded and wiped my nose on my hand. "I thought you wouldn't make it."

"I promised to keep you safe." He slid his right hand up my back, sending a shiver through my body. "Who is that?"

Suddenly I remembered Kole, I pushed away from Folkvarr and ran to Kole. "Help him," I begged, and pressed the apron against his bleeding wounds.

"Who is he?"

"A leshii and the boy who just saved my life."

Folkvarr knelt beside me and took a round jar out of the satchel he carried on his waist. Screwing off the top he said, "Stuff this in the wound. It will stop the bleeding."

I dug my finger into the muddy substance and rubbed it on Kole's cuts. He shivered under my touch. "We have to save him. If he gets a fever . . ."

"What about them? Will they help?"

Will-O-Wisps flew around the tree. "They might. Help me lift him."

We each grabbed one end and carried Kole closer to the trunk of the tree. I laid him against the roots and put my hand on the sacred willow. "Please, save him."

Wisps buzzed around us, swirling the air like tiny snowflakes. One by one they found a spot on Kole. He scrunched his forehead and beads of sweat slid down his face. Wind rustled the long branches of the willow and I held my breath, anxiously waiting.

"What happened?" Folkvarr crouched beside me on the grass, his chest rising and falling as he still caught his breath.

"He took me to the rusalki palace."

"Then you know where my father is?" Folkvarr's voice rose with him, and he smiled. "Show me."

Taking one more glance at Kole, and seeing the Will-O-Wisps tend to his cuts, I led Folkvarr away from the tree. Yes. I knew where the rusalki palace was, but how could we ever go there? "The palace is underwater in a cave, not far from here, but we would never survive the journey."

"Why do you say that?"

"The swim is too far. I don't think any of us would make it

before our breath gave way. Then there's voldak . . . they lie on the floor. Waiting." A chill rushed through me and I hugged myself, remembering the hoard chasing us through the woods.

"Those undead were from there?"

"Yes."

Folkvarr swung one of his axes, pacing back and forth. "How many?"

"Too many to fight, especially under water."

"Then we bring them to the surface."

"What?"

"On land we stand a chance. Once we've dealt with the undead, we can safely make the swim and I can save my father."

"There's too many."

"Then we will find more men. Kiev is only a day's ride. There must be men who will fight against such evil."

I thought to the young priest who had visited our settlement not long ago and my Aunt Jasna. Aunt Jasna had remarried a wealthy merchant after her first husband died. Though, I rarely saw my Uncle Evan due to his time abroad, he had a big circle of powerful friends. Between my Aunt's connections and whatever aid the priests could give, it might be enough.

"There is a group of byzantine priests. They visited our village not long ago, talking about their Christian God. They spoke about fighting evil. I think they would help. Maybe they've dealt with voldak before?"

"Then we leave now."

"Wait." I grabbed Folkvarr's arm. "We can't leave him here."

Folkvarr looked over my shoulder. "As soon as he wakes, we go."

<h1 style="text-align:center">15</h1>

The rain stopped, and we sat amidst the grass waiting for the creature to wake. Agna hadn't told me much else, but I sensed she kept something hidden. She constantly rung her hands in her apron, and watched the woodland spirit with a strange intensity.

"You said you don't think we can make the swim?" I asked.

"Yes." She shifted her body to face me. "When I went in the water—"

"You went in? You could've been killed."

"I know, but I had to be sure Kole spoke truth. The spirits can never be trusted."

"What did you see?"

"A bright light," she said. "So intense it warmed the water, and the outline of the palace."

"Is there another entrance? One closer?"

She shrugged. "There could be, but then why wouldn't he have shown me?"

"You said they cannot be trusted."

"Yes . . . I did." Her gaze lifted to the weeping willow.

"What is it?"

"Nothing."

If she wasn't going to tell me, I wasn't going to ask. I had enough on my mind. How could we swim far? I'm sure I could hold my breath longer than Agna, but not long enough to enter an underwater palace, rescue my father, and return to the surface. Even with the undead taken care of on land, we would still need a way to make it to the palace. Once there, how would we move around? My head spun with question after question and not one answer.

Would Father be angry that we went for him rather than focus on the source of the undead?

What if Father wasn't alive?

The leshii groaned and Agna went to his side.

"Are you feeling better?" she asked.

The wisps danced around his shoulders. He pet one on the head with his finger and smiled. "Almost like myself again." He slid to a sitting position, wincing with the move. He looked over at me, his smile changing into a frown. "Who is that?"

Agna's eyes widened and she immediately stood. "A friend. He saved us."

"Vikings are no friends."

I rose to my feet and slid out my axes. "I could have let the undead kill you."

"Maybe you should have." The boy snarled. His body grew, and black fur sprouted from his skin. Fangs replaced human teeth.

"Wait!" Agna stood in between us, arms out wide. "There is a bigger threat here. You need to work together or our lands will be full with voldak."

Fey approached from the left, growling at the black wolf standing in front of me. I whistled and Fey came to my side. The leshii shifted back into the boy.

"The wolf listens to you."

I wasn't sure if he was asking me a question or stating the truth. "When he wants."

"Kole, Folkvarr is here to help with the undead. He has not harmed anyone, and has protected me more than once."

"Ah, he's the lover then?"

"What?" Agna's face flushed red. "How dare you."

Kole patted her shoulder. "Easy girl. 'Twas a joke."

Satisfied that our woodland spirit meant no harm, Fey relaxed and trotted over to Agna who rubbed behind his ears.

"We need to go to Kiev." I slid my axes back in their holster. "We're not enough to take on the horde."

"We agree there. Care for a ride, *krasavitza moya*?"

Agna stepped away from Kole, her chin held high. "My legs are fine."

"Then lead on." He bowed and I thought Agna might shove her dagger at his grin.

16

olkvarr went to talk with Vega and Flo. While I didn't mind Folkvarr's company, the two men in his party frightened me, especially the one with the markings on his shaved head. It was not my place to say who could go with us to Kiev, but I let Folkvarr know my Aunt Jasna didn't take kindly to the Northmen, and since I would be seeing her first, I thought it best only he come with.

Wind brushed inside as I shut the door to my home.

"You've been gone awhile." Danica leaned over a pot by the oven and blew on the steamy liquid in her ladle. Garlic, potato and thyme filled the room, making my stomach grumble with hunger. I gazed greedily at the pot, wishing there was time to eat.

Taking a steady breath, I twisted my hands in my apron, knowing my next words would most certainly start an argument. I didn't want to fight with my sister, not today. "I'm leaving for Kiev."

"Kiev?"

"Yes. We're going to find a way to kill the voldak."

Danica dropped the ladle and wiped her hands on the rag

we kept by the spices. "Why must you be involved. It's not safe."

"I know . . . but I need to go."

"No," she said. "You want to go. Is *he* going?"

Tears pricked my eyes as I remembered the voldak chasing me in the woods. The hissing and groaning they made, and how each step brought me closer to death. Those sounds would haunt my dreams for eternity. "There were more undead in the woods. They attacked us."

Danica crossed the dirt and grabbed me in a hug. "You shouldn't be helping them. It's too dangerous. Are you all right?"

I gripped her rubaKHa and held on to her embrace, thankful we at least had each other. "Yes. Scared, but I'm okay."

She pulled back, and looked at me from arm's length. "Don't go."

"We're leaving now. Look after Yaya." I turned away, unable to watch the fear and sadness fill her eyes.

"You can't!"

I reached for the door, knowing if I didn't leave quickly, Danica would cause a fit.

"They can't be trusted," she argued, holding her hand against the door. "*He* can't be trusted."

"He's different," I whispered, gently pushing her aside and opening the door. A rush of cold air swept into the room.

"Did you forget what his people did to our parents?"

"No, I could never." I grabbed the handle. "Be safe sister, and don't forget the porridge—you know how much Grandfather hates it salted."

I didn't dare meet Danica's hateful gaze as I closed the door behind me.

Folkvarr stood outside with two brown mares, Fey by his side.

"Are you ready?" he asked.

"Where did you get two horses?" Our settlement only had a handful of horses. We didn't travel much, and with Kiev only a day's walk, we didn't need them.

"We're borrowing them."

I grabbed the reins of the horse and pulled myself into the saddle. Kole had disappeared and I wondered if he flew above us as a bird, or stalked the woods as the black wolf.

We rode in silence. Fey running beside us. Several times I glanced over at Folkvarr as we rode. His face stern, eyes never straying from the path ahead. His silence was more terrifying than his anger.

Did he think about what happened in the glade? Or after? My mind thought back to Folkvarr holding me. His rough hands on my waist. His breath on my neck. Everything inside me tingled and buzzed with the desire for him to touch me again.

Was I wrong for wanting a Viking?

How could I want anyone so quickly?

The longing to have Folkvarr hold me rumbled inside me like the river. Great and roaring.

Danica would never allow it.

Though it had been months since I last saw Aunt Jasna, I knew she would slay him with her sword if he even glanced at me with want. A Viking murdered Mama, her sister.

Cautiously, I glanced to my right, my stomach fluttering with curiosity and desire.

Folkvarr turned his head as if he felt the want between us.

His stormy eyes sparkled with intensity, and the corner of his mouth slightly curved into a smile.

Heat flooded my cheeks, and in that wild moment, I knew we were both in terrible, wonderful, trouble.

17

didn't want to stop, but the horses needed to rest. Agna and I sat by the fire, silent. Between the undead, and my father, my head held so many questions it ached.

My father was the strongest of all of us. He could swing his axe in one hand and take two men down with the other. I had seen him fight four men at once, roaring like a lion. Even a gash to his arm would not slow him. Men followed him, respected him, as not only a man of his word, but courageous enough to stand against other Northmen who would continue the fight between the Slavs and our people. Rurik, and he shared the same vision: a land where we could be prosperous, and trade instead of pillage.

But trade was where my father's generosity ended.

"Would you like some cheese?" Agna said, the fire between us.

I shook my head.

"Very well. I'll save your portion for the morning." She

tucked the cheese back into her pack and drank from the water skin.

"Where's Fey?" Agna looked around at the empty stretch of land. "And Kole?"

"Off to hunt." The spirit had run with Fey in his wolf form, and who knew where the two had disappeared to. Watching Kole's transformation into a beast stirred many thoughts in my mind. Our gods hadn't blessed our men with shapeshifting, did that make them less powerful? None could be more powerful than Odin, yet, I had not seen Odin's great powers at work.

Agna brushed dirt off her apron, trying to clean the spots that now speckled it. Flames danced around her cheeks, and the green in her eyes sparkled with wildness. Did she know about the water maidens? Was it a lure to kill us? Is that why she relived herself and left us?

No. She was not like the others, and I would not dishonor her by thinking so.

"What is it?" she asked.

"Nothing."

"It's not nothing. Do you want to talk?"

"How did those maidens overcome my father?"

"I don't know what kinds of creatures reside in your lands, but here," her voice trailed off into a whisper, "here live many unexplainable things."

Agna breathed in and played with the string hanging from her belt. "As children, we are told of the spirits, ones who play tricks, ones who live in the forest, homes, and barns, and ones to never anger or search for. I never truly believed all of

Yaya's tales, until now." She stared at me, her eyes filling with tears. "I've never seen anything so terrifying. All the times I've played by the river, taunting the warnings." A tear dropped and she wiped it away with her pointer finger. "My heart breaks for your loss, and I promise I will help you find an end to those devils in the river."

Her tears slipped, one after the other. She quickly brushed them away as if embarrassed. Our people were bound for hatred, yet she showed none.

I wanted to take her in my arms and kiss the tears away. When she looked at me, her bottom lip wet with sadness, I wanted to rip off the scarf keeping her hair in place, and throw those damned temple rings into the river. Her hair was too beautiful to be hidden behind cloth. I wanted to feel the silky strands between my fingers.

My father's words racked my head with warning, but I couldn't heed them.

Agna was not like other Slavs.

Fey returned with a rabbit in his mouth and dropped it by Agna's feet. She jumped, breaking our connection. "Good boy."

Fey circled around before finding a spot beside her, and curled into a ball.

Agna pulled her dagger out and grabbed the rabbit by its feet.

"Let me." I moved to sit next to her and held out my hand.

When she hesitated, I said, "It will ease my mind."

She handed me the rabbit and I took out my knife.

Agna yawned. Her eyes fluttered.

"If you're tired, rest."

"No, I'm fine." She yawned again, stretching out her arms.

"Rest," I said again.

She nodded then curled beside Fey.

As I skinned the rabbit, low breaths left her sleeping lips, the tiniest snores escaping. So fragile, yet brave enough to fight the undead and help save my father.

"Tell me, Viking, why are you here?"

I flinched at the leshii's sudden appearance.

"Will you not share a simple conversation with a fellow?" The boy sat with his legs crossed and chest bare. He reminded me of the wild youth from the woods who would watch us from the shadows and throw sticks to taunt us.

"You are no fellow nor man," I spat back.

Kole grinned. "I am many things."

His wily stare grated on my nerves. "We were sent by our chieftain to investigate the rumors of dead Vikings rising from the dead."

The black in Kole's eyes burned red. "Your people have brought this curse upon us."

Taking the knife, I shanked off the rabbit's fur, glaring at the thing across from me. "*My* people would never deal in dark magic. We respect the gods and the order. To roam undead is a fate no Viking desires. I would not wish it on my enemy."

We glared at one another in an eerie silence.

"I believe you," Kole said, his grin vanishing. "But once this threat is gone. You need to leave."

"I never planned on staying."

Agna whimpered in her sleep, tossing under the blanket. I waited to see if peace would find her again. The blanket fell away and she shivered. I placed the rabbit on a piece of cloth, before reaching over to Agna. I pulled the blanket back over her shoulders. Her brow scrunched as if demons plagued her dreams.

"Hmpf."

I glanced over at Kole who was grinning, again.

"I don't think you'll go anywhere." He shifted into a wolf and raced off into the night.

Agna rolled to her side and curled against my leg. She gripped the side of my pants, digging her face into it. The tension in her brow faded and a soft sigh left her lips.

My heart beat at her touch.

Deep within my soul, I understood more than I would ever admit aloud.

Agna had whittled into my heart.

Kole was right.

I did not want to leave.

18

It had been two years since I'd last seen Kiev. The stonemasons hammered away at the outer wall circling the great city by the river, continuing the work they started so many years ago. I marveled at all the new thatched homes and buildings. A dirt road wound its way around the city and up the hill.

"Go, but stay near the city," Folkvarr told Fey. The gray wolf trotted into the distance.

"I'll join him," Kole said, before shifting into the wolf and dashing off with Fey.

No matter how many times he transformed, I still could not get used to the fantastical sight. How I longed to be able to fly into the sky or dive far below the river's surface. All the things Kole could do, and yet he preferred to annoy my people instead.

Folkvarr and I walked through the main gate. Carts carrying carrots, potatoes and hay passed us by. My aunt and uncle lived on the east end of the city. Aunt Jasna had made a name for herself by weaving beautiful scarves, even the

Turkish merchants coveted them.

My last visit with Aunt Jasna hadn't gone well. She wanted my sister and I to convince Yaya to live in the city, but we all loved our log home in the quiet woods. Other than the memory of our parents, we had no reason to leave.

Folkvarr glared at our surroundings. His jaw clenched and he grasped the twin axes hanging from his belt. The only way I could help him was to find answers, and I prayed to the gods, Aunt Jasna would have them.

Before I knocked on her door, I glanced at Folkvarr. Between the black raven tattoo on his neck, and striking appearance, he resembled a Viking. I thought of leaving him outside, but this was his fight too.

"Cover yourself," I said. "My Aunt doesn't look kindly on Vikings."

He lifted the hood of his cloak over his head, shielding his face with shadows.

I took a deep breath and knocked on the door. Feet shuffled inside, and I knotted my hands in my apron, patiently waiting for Aunt Jasna to open.

"Who's there?" she called from inside.

"It's me, Agna."

The door bolted open. "Agna!" She threw her arms around me, crushing me in a tight embrace. "Come in."

She ushered me into her home. A section to the right had been cleared and all her sewing tools organized on a wooden cart. Scarves matching the brilliant colors of the rainbow, hung from hooks on the wall. To the left lay a wooden bed, a table and chairs, and a fire spit to cook in.

Folkvarr closed the door behind us, but stayed near the entrance.

"What brings you to Kiev? I've missed you, and Danica. And how is Yaya? I keep telling her to live in the city. Why must she be so stubborn?"

Aunt Jasna's bubbly nature brought a smile to my face. Her long blonde hair reminded me of Mama's, and we had the same soft green eyes. Danica more resembled Papa with the same blonde hair, but deep brown eyes.

"It's good to see you too." I smiled, attempting to hide the nervous flutters battering my stomach.

"Who's your friend?" She peered around me to glance at Folkvarr.

Folkvarr shifted on his feet, his gaze darting to me.

"His name is Folkvarr. I hired him to escort me to Kiev."

"Welcome," she said to Folkvarr then looked back to me. "It is good to see you, Agna." She squeezed my hands and pulled me to sit with her at the table.

"You already said that."

"I know." She laughed. "But it *is* good to see you. I was planning to come for you. I have wonderful news."

Come for me?

Her smile widened. "I found a suitor for you."

"What?" I pulled away from her grasp. "What are you talking about?"

"Now, Agna. We spoke about this." She leaned back, folding her arms, pursing her lips and speaking to me like a child. "You and your sister cannot stay in the settlement, alone, and unwed. The merchant I do business with has a son who secks a bride. We've got the dowry all set. He's a wonderful young man and will treat you well."

"No." I stood, pushing the chair away. "I won't do it."

Aunt Jasna rolled her eyes, and stood with me. "Enough of this. The arrangement is set. Next full moon you will wed here."

She acted as if marrying a stranger were a simple chore.

"I won't!" I backed away from her and bumped into Folkvarr. During the conversation, he had moved closer to me. Feeling his body against mine, strengthened me. "You can't make me."

"Don't act like a child." She put one hand on her hip and wagged a finger in my face. "You are my responsibility and I will not let my sister's legacy die in the woods. Either you come willingly or I take you."

Folkvarr stepped in front of me. "No, you won't."

"It's fine," I said, tugging on his arm. "Let's just go."

Aunt Jasna squinted in disgust at Folkvarr. "Hired help should mind their manners. This is between Agna and me."

"We're leaving." I pulled Folkvarr back, and when I did, his hood fell away, revealing his face and the black markings on his neck.

"A Viking! In my home! What is this Agna?" Aunt Jasna dashed to the fire spit and grabbed a sword.

"He's a friend." I stepped in between them, holding out my hands to stop her.

"Get away from her!" She pointed her sword at Folkvarr.

"Aunt Jasna!"

She held the sword with both hands. "Step away from him."

My heart sank. "Please. If you'll just listen."

"Murderers," she hissed. "That's what your kind are. A plague infesting our land."

Folkvarr stood still, his hands resting on the tips of his axes.

"We're leaving." I tugged Folkvarr to the door. "And I am not marrying anyone."

With that, I ripped open the door and ran, Folkvarr right behind me. I didn't know where to run, so I kept making turns until my Aunt Jasna's screaming pleas disappeared.

"She's not following," Folkvarr huffed.

We slowed, and hid behind a wooden home. I leaned over my thighs, catching my breath.

"I won't marry him," I panted. "I won't."

How could she do this to me? She doesn't visit for months, and when I finally see her, she tells me I'm to a wed a stranger? Panic clenched my throat, clawing at my insides.

"Speak with Yaya." Folkvarr touched my shoulder, forcing me to look at him. "She'll listen."

I bit my lip in attempt to hold the tears back. Marry? How could I marry a stranger? I didn't want to be with someone who didn't know me. Someone who didn't love me. Someone who didn't make me feel safe.

Folkvarr gently squeezed my shoulder and the compassion in his stormy eyes melted me. His gaze went to my lips, and the desire to feel his skin against mine removed any other thought I had. We both straightened, moving together and closer at the same time as if a string pulled us together. He crushed me against the wall and leaned over me.

"Say the word, and I promise you will not be forced to

marry anyone you don't want." His soft lips beckoned a response from me, but I was frozen beneath his breath.

I opened my mouth to speak, to say anything, but words failed.

He dragged his thumb across my lips. I closed my eyes, losing myself in his touch. He moved his thumb down my chin, down my neck, until I opened my eyes and begged him to kiss me.

Like the mighty wind, he rushed into me. Tender lips too soft for a rough boy like him. He tasted of mint and bright morning skies. Sensation after sensation rolled through me like the river. Tossing me under its waves and carrying me into a land unknown.

Folkvarr left my lips, kissing my neck, and growling when I tilted my head back. He tugged at the apron covering my rubaKHa, pulling at the fabric keeping us separated.

Heat covered me in a flame. My mind drifted to the skies.

In all my dreams of kissing a boy, never had I imagined it would feel like this. My mind lost itself within the kiss. Nothing mattered. Not the undead. Not my Aunt Jasna. Nothing.

Warmth spread through my body, making me dizzy, and longing for more.

Our lips found each other again, and Folkvarr lifted me off the ground. He dug his hands under my dress as he pressed me against the wall. My chest pounded. My clothes constricted me. I wanted it off. All of it.

He slipped his hands underneath my rubaKHa, and the moment he touched my thighs, I wanted to explode. I grabbed his hair, pulling him closer and deeper into our kiss. My body tingled. My mind raced. Sweat slid down my neck.

Kiss after kiss, he traveled across my face and neck. Wind touched my skin as he lifted my dress higher, traveling where no boy had gone before. He dug his fingers into my backside and my breath hitched in my throat.

"Wait!" I broke the kiss and tried to steady my mind from the whirlwind I was becoming lost in.

He breathed heavily, then froze as if he realized how far and fast we were moving.

I leaned my head back against the wood, knowing if I made eye contact, any willpower I had would break.

This is madness. And yet, all I could think of was kissing him again, and again and again. How I never wanted to stop.

Slowly, he released me, my dress falling back into place. With his head hung low, he whispered, "I'm sorry. I just . . ." He turned away from me, severing the moment.

"No." I pulled him back. "It's fine. I don't think either of us planned that." I stood on my tiptoes to kiss him.

He carefully kissed me back before breaking away. "You drive me mad."

I smiled at the grin on his face. "Mad with desire?"

"You're going to get me into a lot of trouble." The grin he wore widened into a big smile, displaying two perfect dimples.

"I think we're both in trouble."

And we were. Deep, roaring, trouble.

A cart rolled by the adjacent path, reminding me of our main purpose for coming here. Folkvarr raised his hood, disappearing again beneath the folds of fabric.

"I don't think your aunt will help us. What about the priest you mentioned?" Folkvarr placed a hand on my back as we walked, treating me like precious cargo he couldn't bear to part with.

Near the top of the hill against the far right wall sat a wooden hut with a circular roof. Smoke puffed out of the top and a wooden cross rested against the front side wall. I stopped in front of the cross, my heart doing a strange pitter- patter.

"I've heard only little about the Christian God." Folkvarr spoke in a low tone as if even mentioning the name would invoke the wrath of his own gods.

"I always believed in Perun and the spirits, but after meeting Kole and seeing the voldak, I am afraid to see any other being."

"Do not fear," Folkvarr said, leaning by my ear. "None of those lesser gods can compare to the might of Odin who watches over us now."

There was no reason to discuss the nature of gods with Folkvarr. We believed very differently. Odin had not made his presence known. To me, he was just a tale the Vikings believed. Though, after seeing the undead, I believed anything possible.

Folkvarr took the lead, crossing over the wooden threshold. I walked close behind, rubbing my hands together. Candles lit the corners, and four wooden benches sat neatly in rows. A boy stood at a podium with a feather in his hands. He wore his brown hair cropped closely to his face. It matched the shade of his long robe which had a red and black brocade around the hem.

He smiled at our approach. "Good morrow, friends."

I gripped the back of Folkvarr's cloak, suddenly nervous to be in the presence of this young priest. A wooden cross that matched the one outside dangled from a rope around his neck.

"Have you come for guidance?" he asked, walking around the post he stood by.

"Of a sort," Folkvarr replied.

The priest smiled and waved a hand at the bench. "Sit, and we shall speak."

His smooth voice held no anger, no judgment. He looked at Folkvarr and me as if we were both young children eager to hear a story. Finding my courage, I released my hold on Folkvarr and approached the bench. Folkvarr chose to stand.

I sat at the end of the same bench the priest sat on. "We have come for aid," I said. "There are voldak in our woods."

"Voldak?"

"Dead men who walk." Folkvarr moved to stand closer to us.

The priest's brow narrowed. "You have seen these abominations?"

"Aye," Folkvarr said. "I have fought them twice."

"These are indeed dark times." The priest's voice lowered. "My name is Caspian."

"I'm Agna and he is Folkvarr."

"I wish we were meeting under different circumstances." He smiled at me, his dark eyes full of concern.

"Will you help?" I watched his expression for confirmation.

"I will." He stood. "There are three other priests here, but all are out. I expect one of my brothers to return in two days' time."

"We can't wait that long." Folkvarr moved toward the priest. "There is a horde, and they must be stopped before more people die."

Caspian's mouth hung open, dazed for a moment, before

he snapped it shut and nodded. "Then I will go with you now. I must leave a letter for my brothers and tell them of this dark news." Caspian rushed to the podium and took a feather in his hands.

"Where are these undead?" He glanced between Folkvarr and me as he dipped the feather tip into a black vial.

"My settlement is one day's walk, east, near the Dnieper River."

He scribbled on a piece of tan material. "I will let my brothers know so they may bring help when they return. I'll need to collect some supplies for the journey."

"Thank you," I said.

Folkvarr tugged on my arm, pulling me aside. "What of the spirit boy?"

I knew very little of the Christian God and the beliefs. We needed the priest's help, and I couldn't have Kole scaring him away. "I will go speak with him now. He must stay as a boy and not transform. Meet me outside with the priest."

"Wait." Folkvarr gripped my arm. "We should leave together."

I placed my hand over his. "I'll be fine."

Our gazes stayed on one another. His rough fingers brought warmth where they touched my skin. I sensed through his touch he didn't want me to leave. Unspoken words flew between us, emotions tying us in this strange dream where dead walked and my companion came in the form of my most hated foe. He glided his other hand over mine.

"I can go with you," he whispered. "We can tell the priest where to meet us."

In our silence, we had inched closer. The breath from his

words cascaded over my face. Within his blue eyes, specks of yellow and gray danced around the black centers, swirling me into a daze.

"Kole may not show right away if you're there. Make sure the priest comes." I slid out of Folkvarr's grasp, his expression furrowing.

"We should be together."

My heart pattered at his choice of words.

"Stay together," he corrected. "It's safer."

"It is," I replied, doing my best to ignore what we both had heard. "But we need the priest. We can't have some silly spirit scaring away the help."

A smile tugged at Folkvarr's lips. "Go, I will meet you outside the gates."

I smiled back, holding his gaze once more, before I turned and left.

19

gna disappeared around the turn. The red of her dress, the last fleeting image. *We should* be *together*. The words slipped out, and she kindly ignored them, but we both had heard it. I leaned against the wall, breathing away the desire that still pumped through me. I couldn't believe I had almost bed her right there on the side of the road. We were hidden, but still, she wasn't some wench.

The honey taste of her lips still lingered on mine.

She was breathtakingly beautiful. Beautiful enough to drive me away from my home and into her arms. What future would we have though? Her aunt planned her marriage, and my father would never allow our union.

And what of the rest of our people?

Father and I had visited many settlements since we left Novgorod, and received almost the same response in every one: cold glares, whispers in our passing, and sometimes, on the rare occasion we offended someone, an arrow in our direction.

It would take years for the Slavs hatred and fear to finally fade. Even if I wanted to be with Agna, our clans would never allow it. If she came to Novgorod, where our people began to mix and live, *maybe* it could work. But would she leave with me?

Knocking my head back against the building, I looked up at the cloudless sky.

How I felt about Agna didn't matter. I had two tasks: slaughter the horde and save my father.

"I'm ready." Caspian carried a cloth bag across his shoulder.

"Then we go." I pushed off the wall, eager to leave the city. "Our horses are outside the gate."

"Tell me more about your encounters with the undead."

As we walked to the gates, I recited the first morning we fought them. How they moved with wit, and never slowed until they were chopped to pieces or their heads were removed. I described the horde, but left out the part of the willow. If I had not seen it with my own eyes, I would never believe a tree could root itself out of the ground and fight.

Agna waited outside with the horses. Kole nowhere to be seen. "Agna will ride with me," I said to Caspian. "Take the other horse."

Caspian nodded and said hello to Agna. I grabbed the reins from her. "Where is he," I whispered.

"He went ahead. Said he would meet us later back at the settlement." She stepped onto the stirrup, and I held her waist, helping her into the saddle. Once seated, I climbed behind her.

She wiggled around, trying to get comfortable. The shuffling of her body against mine sent a surge of wanting through my thoughts.

"Here." Holding her waist, I pulled her back into my lap, adjusting her until her body molded against mine perfectly. I was keenly aware of the lavender scent of her skin as if she'd bathed in a pool of it.

With the reins in my hand, I urged the horse forward. When our speed increased, I switched the reins to my right hand and wrapped my left arm around her. We rode through the afternoon and most of the night, resting only once for the horses. By the time we reached the settlement, dawn had broken over the trees.

"We're here," I said, softly.

Agna had fallen asleep during the last part of the ride, laying her head back against my chest. She yawned and rubbed her eyes, slowly lifting away from me. "How long did I sleep?"

"Not long enough."

She dismounted first.

"Go home and rest," I said, getting off the horse. "We'll meet at dusk. The priest won't do us much good if he's not awake to fight."

"I'll come to the longhouse later." She held my gaze as she spoke.

I nodded and broke the connection before her green eyes completely took hold of me. "Come," I said to Caspian as he yawned a goodbye to Agna. "We will plan first, then rest."

He nodded, yawning again. I wondered if the boy would even be able to fight. He carried no visible weapons, and seemed too innocent to shed blood, and much too frail to have any true strength.

Vega and Flo sat around the pit fire, Flo sharpening his

sword and Vega chewing on a chunk of bread. Both quickly stood as the priest and I entered.

"Where are the men?" Vega asked. He glared at Caspian. "Who is this?"

"I am Caspian. I've—"

"He's a priest," I interrupted and stepped in front of Caspian. "He can help with the undead."

Flo tapped his blade against his open palm. "Can he? Without a sword?"

"I have other means to battle." Caspian puffed out his chest, though it did little to make him tougher. "Our order has encountered undead before."

"You've killed them?" Bits of bread flew out of Vega's mouth as he examined our newest companion.

"No . . . No, I haven't, but I've trained."

"What is this?" Flo laughed, and turned to me. "This is the best you could do? Tsk Tsk."

"We are not welcomed in Kiev, or any other nearby territory," I argued back. "I brought who I could."

"Don't forget about me."

Kole leaned against the wood entrance, smirking, with his arms folded across his chest.

"And who are you?" Flo was the first to ask and move closer to the door.

"An ally." Kole sauntered over to the fire pit. "Arguing is wasting time. Shall we talk about how we are going to attack a horde of undead?"

"Aye." Vega nodded, followed by Flo and me.

We sat around the pit, all of us waiting for Kole to speak.

"The horde consists of thirty undead. There may be more, but last I saw they numbered thirty."

"Six for each of us, if the priest is of any use." Flo spit into the fire and the flames crackled.

"Luring the horde out will be easy," Kole continued. "One of us will swim down, and draw them to the surface. Once the horde is dealt with the passage to the rusalki palace will be clear."

"Then we save my father."

"Do we know if Holemgeiir lives?" Vega asked Kole.

"He lives," I said. Though I had no solid proof, I knew my father lived. He had to be alive.

"What can you do, priest?" Flo laid his sword across his lap.

I eyed Caspian, waiting for him to answer. During our journey here, I mentioned the horde and how my father had been kidnapped to an underwater palace. Surprisingly, the priest accepted the story with only few questions. It made me wonder what creatures he had seen in his own travels.

"I have spells," said Caspian.

"You are a witch?" Flo's head tilted to the side.

"No," Caspian replied. "These are holy spells, granted from God."

Vega huffed. "If you play with magic, you are a witch, regardless of what god gave you the power."

Kole watched the exchange. I couldn't decipher his stoic expression. I knew he was a creature who hated my people. Did he hate the Christians too? I didn't trust Kole, though I gauged he did not like voldak in his woods. I wanted to ask him if he could call on more of his kind, but that was a conversation needed to be held elsewhere.

"When do we attack?" I wanted to leave now, but the undead wouldn't leave with the sun out.

"Tonight," Kole said. "Rest now. We leave after dusk."

"I'll be back," I said, standing. "Caspian, you may rest here. You two," I said pointing to Flo and Vega. "Be nice to the priest, otherwise we each have to kill ten."

Vega laughed. "An easy task!"

Flo said something, but I was already walking toward the door.

Agna nearly crashed into me as I stepped outside.

"Sorry!" she said.

I grabbed her elbow, steadying her. "My fault."

She nodded. Her cheeks flushed red. "Are you leaving?"

Why did she refuse to meet my eyes? "Not now. We leave after dusk."

"So soon?" She looked up, and her eyes watered. "What's going to happen? I need to get Yaya . . . and my sister . . . and."

"Hey." I held her arms which were tight at her sides as she twisted her apron. "The horde will be nowhere near here. The fight will be out there."

"There were so many . . ." Her voice drifted and I knew she thought back to that day when she had laid eyes on the horde.

Footsteps clanked behind me. I glanced back and saw Flo watching us.

"Let's walk." I guided her away from the longhouse and away from Flo. Just like my father, Flo would not approve of mingling with the Slavs. It was one thing to sleep with one, but another to feel anything more, and I wanted more than just a night with Agna.

We walked down the hill and through the main path of the settlement. Slavs were out, milling about. More than one looked at Agna and me, until I glared back and they lowered their heads.

"I need to tell Yaya about tonight." Agna started toward Yaya's hut.

"I'll go with you."

She nodded, and we began a silent journey to her grandmother's house. Fey darted beside me, finally showing himself.

"Where have you been?" I asked.

He shook out his fur, and rubbed against Agna's leg like a dog. She whispered something in her language, and patted his head.

Yaya was by Lew's gate, feeding the ram a potato.

Agna dashed to her side and wrapped her in a hug.

"Oh, child. What bothers you now?"

"We plan to fight the horde tonight," I said.

Yaya nodded. "I see. So the time has come."

"Yaya, you must come to the village and stay with us." Agna released her hold on Yaya, but begged her with her eyes.

"My place is here. I will be safe."

"Why must you be so stubborn?" Agna glared at her grandmother.

"Agna." I kept my voice even. "If Yaya says she will be safe, trust her."

"You don't even know her." Agna swirled to face me. "It's always been her way. All the time." Agna balled her fists. "Stay here then," she said to Yaya. "I have to protect Danica. Since you won't."

Agna shoved past me. Yaya made no move to follow, but I saw the sadness sag her shoulders. I gave a quick nod to Yaya, and dashed after Agna.

"Agna!" I called as she sprinted through the forest. Her red dress whipping past the green. "Agna!"

The more I yelled, the faster she ran. I pumped my legs faster, gaining ground. Her dress snagged on a thorn bush and she screamed, pulling at the stuck fabric.

"*Oh, blin!*" She yanked harder, and thorns scratched at her hands.

"Stop." I reached her, and pushed her hands out of the way. The thorn bush had embedded itself into her clothes. Slowly, I picked each thorn off and broke the branches.

Agna breathed heavy, her face flushing red.

I ripped the last thorn out. "There."

"Thank you." Still out of breath, she smoothed her dress. Blood trickled from the scratches on her hands.

"Here." I took her hands, examining them for splinters. She winced as I ripped more than one from her palm. "Why are you angry with Yaya?"

When she met my gaze, her lower lip trembled. Holding her hands, I gently pressed them against my shirt, trying to staunch the blood.

"I don't want her to die."

One tear slipped down her cheek. I wanted to kiss it. Instead, I shifted her hands in my left and with my right thumb, brushed the sadness away. "Shall I go back and remove her by force?"

She let out a small laugh. "No. I'm sure no one can move

Yaya. Where do you think Lew gets his stubbornness?"

I laughed and she laughed again.

"If I had the men to spare, I would send one to guard her."

Agna nodded. "I know. I can't lose her too. Ever since my parents died, she refuses to come to the village, like it's cursed."

Seeing the hopelessness drag her smile down, I brought her bloody hands to my lips. "Tomorrow at dawn, this nightmare will end."

"We still need to rescue your father."

"Yes, but the voldak will be gone and you will be safe."

"Folkvarr . . . I know," she met my gaze and my chest beat. "I know the history between our people is filled with anger and violence, but you've shown me that a name does not define you."

Still holding her hands, I gripped them tighter, anxious at what her next words would be.

"You are different, and I . . ." She stumbled over her words, and I swore the green in her eyes pulsed with beauty. "I am glad to know you."

Red flushed into her cheeks, brightening them into a rose hue I wanted to caress. Wetness painted her bottom lip. I couldn't stop myself from thinking of how she tasted like honey.

"I am glad to know you too." My voice cracked with hoarseness, and when her gaze went to my lips, I knew she wanted to kiss me.

I would not deny her.

With a gentle touch, I pulled her hands to my chest, bringing her closer. I paused, wanting to say something, but words left my mind, every one useless.

"Isn't this sweet."

Kole leaned against a nearby tree. Agna, quickly stepped away from me, so quickly as if the mere sight of us together would anger the gods.

"What do you want, spirit?" Another interruption and Kole would learn how good I was with an axe.

"Making sure you stay focused." The red in his coal eyes crackled like lightning. "If you plan on fighting the horde, you'll need your rest."

Growling, I whipped out my axes. "Don't order me around."

"Boys." Agna stepped in between us. "Fighting amongst ourselves will not help us win." She placed a hand on my chest. "We should return, and prepare."

I slipped the axes back into their holder. "Then let us be gone."

She tugged on my arm, dragging me away from the spirit creature who snarled at our departure. If the opportunity arose during our battle, I would take him down.

He would never interrupt Agna and me again.

20

"Bar the door," Folkvarr said. "We don't know whether the horde will stay contained. Stay inside." I nodded. "We will. Be safe."We shared a long silence as if the words hung in the air and neither I nor him could capture them. If my sister didn't stand behind us, I knew he would've kissed me. I wanted him to kiss me.

"I will be back," he said softly with a determined look in his eye.

"I know."

He closed the door and I shoved the wooden plank in place. I stood there, unable to tear myself away. My heart thumped, pleading with me to run after him and yell at this foolish plan. Folkvarr would be the one to draw the voldak out of the water and lure them to a place he and the other men had a better chance at fighting them.

Why did he have to be so stubborn, and bull headed, just like Lew. Why not someone else take the risk? Why him?

I didn't want him to die.

"Do you want to play knucklebones?" Danica gave a soft smile. "There is nothing for us to do but wait."

Glancing at the door, I nodded. I couldn't go after Folkvarr. I had to believe in him and the others. With the help of a leshii and the priest, they had a chance.

Joining my sister at the table, she pulled out five sheep knuckles. "Want to go first?"

I nodded and grabbed the knuckles. She smiled, and I tossed the pieces into the air and quickly turned my hand over to catch them.

Only two landed.

"My turn!" She grabbed the knuckles and tossed them up.

How could I sit and play a game when Folkvarr was out there risking his life? "I'm going to make tea."

Leaving the game, I went to the stove and put the old kettle on. The fire from supper still burned. I opened the chest of herbs and searched for the valerian root. I needed to relax.

"Here." Danica moved beside me, grabbing a bottle.

"Thanks."

I let Danica make the tea, and sat by the table, trying not to think of Folkvarr. How I wished that raven on his neck would come alive and protect him.

"I saw Aunt Jasna," I said, turning my mind from what was happening in the woods. "She found a suitor for me."

"From where?" The edge in Danica's voice filled me with relief.

"Some merchant's son. She said I have no choice to marry."

Folkvarr's words flooded my heart, *Say the word and I promise you will not marry anyone you don't want to.*

"You shouldn't be forced, but you know we can't live like this forever." Danica placed the tea in front of me.

"You agree with her?" I sipped the warm tea, letting it relax the tightness in my shoulders.

"No." Danica tapped her finger against the cup in her hands. "But, maybe it's a good thing. Won't you at least meet the boy?"

No. I glanced away from her dark eyes that searched mine.

"Is there someone else?" Her question stirred too many emotions. I couldn't tell her about Folkvarr. Not now. Maybe not ever.

Maybe Yaya would understand. When this was over, I'd talk to her, tell her I didn't want to marry a stranger. Danica wanted the best for me, like I did for her. She would want me to marry for love, like our parents had. Our parents loved each other until their last moments. I wanted that type of forever.

"Your hair's a mess." Danica pulled off my handkerchief and unhooked the temple rings. "When was the last time you brushed it?"

"At least I remembered to wash the porridge off my teeth."

She laughed and ran the comb through my tangled knots. The smooth strokes made my eyes flutter with sleep. I reached up and touched her arm. "Thank you. Lately, you've been more of a big sister than me."

"Someone has to look out for you." She tousled my hair before going back to bringing the comb through it.

Scrape.

"Did you hear that?" My ears perked at the noise.

"Maybe Grandfather is hungry," Danica replied.

The house spirit never made any strange noises, and especially ones from outside.

Scrape. Scrape.

Thud.

"I heard that." Danica dropped the comb and we both moved back near the stove.

Thud. Thud.

The door moved, groaning against the wooden plank. I grabbed the dagger Folkvarr had given me and held it in between both hands. Danica grasped the back of my arms as she hid behind me. Our breaths sounding too loud for the night.

THUD.

We screamed as the door shoved, but the plank held.

"Whatever it is, they can't get in," I assured her.

Something scampered on the walls. Dirt fell from the ceiling. Footsteps. I couldn't tell whether they were one set or more, pounded on the roof.

They couldn't get it in. The roof . . . the leak!

"Danica, watch—"

The roof collapsed and with it came a man.

"No, it can't be." My hands shook and I gripped the dagger tighter.

"Papa?" Danica stepped around me.

"Hellooo, my beloveds."

Papa, dead many years, stood before us. The clothes we buried him in hung around his body, tattered and barely holding on. His strong face had withered to a pale corpse. Purple bruising covered the right side of his face. The white of his eyes bright against the red pupils. Besides the discoloration of his skin, and the red eyes, he *looked* like Papa.

"I . . . have . . . returned." The words were garbled and dragged out of his mouth, sending a chill across my spine.

"Papa died long ago." I had to remind myself this creature of the dead was not him.

"Papa? Is it really you?" Danica stepped closer, her hands stretched out, and a strange wild glassiness tainted her eyes.

"No!" I grabbed her arm. "He is not Papa!"

"Little sparrow." The voldak smiled at Danica and held out his arms. "I have come to protect you."

Danica's eyes glistened and she smiled. "You came for us? You knew what was happening."

"Danica, no. He speaks lies!"

"You're wrong," Danica said with a twisted smile. "He's come back. He's finally come back."

Before she could get any closer, I charged at the voldak, raising my dagger to plunge into his already dead heart. He swung around just as I came in, and backhanded me across the room. I slammed into the door.

"Papa!" Danica screamed. "What are you doing?"

I shook the dizziness from my head and scrambled to grab the dagger I'd dropped.

"I will keep you safe," he groaned, stomping toward me. He grabbed me by the front of my rubaKHa and lifted me off my feet. "She will not interfcre."

I scratched at his hands, desperately trying to get out of his grasp. With a forceful shove, he pushed me through the wooden door, flinging me outside. Ringing sounded in my head. He walked back inside, and I fought to keep my eyes open.

"Run, Danica!"

My voice croaked and I screamed again, slowly pushing off the ground. Danica screamed. The fear in her voice rose me to my feet. Breathing heavily, I limped to the doorway. My body aching and straining, every muscle screaming at me to stop.

Papa held Danica's limp body in his arms. Her glazed eyes fixed on me as he fed from her neck.

With the dagger secured in my grip I dashed forward and drove it into his head. He howled and released Danica who crumbled to the floor. He turned to me, hissing and spitting black bile. Hands reached forward clawing at my face and I kicked him back, but not before he punched me in the mouth.

I fell back, tripping over my feet while the voldak hissed one last time and stopped moving.

Shallow breaths left Danica's lips and I crawled to her side. "Please, be okay."

I sat beside her, stroking the side of her face. Two large puncture wounds adorned her neck, blood tricking from both.

"I can't lose you, please, Danica. I can't lose you." I held her hand, crying, and wishing morning would come soon.

21

Seven of us entered the woods: Vega and Flo, the priest, Kole, Juri's man Belbog, and one brave soul from the settlement. Seven men against thirty undead. I did not fear death, or the death of my brethren, but the voldak unsettled me. Men that should be in the ground, and passed on, walked with dead eyes and enough wit to raise a sword and strike.

Men who could not feel pain.

Branches and leaves crushed under our boots, and not even Vega spoke on the way. Kole led us through the woods, the sun now disappeared into her nest, and the haunting mist swimming under our feet. The mist lingered, and clung to my boots. I was thankful for the bit of light the moon provided. While the torches we now held would direct us to the cave Kole had spoken of, we couldn't hold a torch and a sword during a fight.

Fey trotted beside me, quiet, as if he sensed the foreboding in the mist.

We passed the great willow and the moon shone brighter around the great tree. If we retreated there, I was sure the ancient being would protect us once again, but I did not want to risk bringing the fire near those leaves.

Caspian whispered prayers as we walked, holding a wooden cross. He carried only one weapon, a flail he'd taken out of his bag. Smaller than the ones I had seen in combat, but I was sure just as dangerous. The spikes on the dangling heads shone under the moonlight.

We had to be enough.

Kole stopped and held a finger to his lips then waved me forward.

My turn.

We had discussed who would lure out the horde. According to Kole, it had to be a Viking, and I was the fastest runner. But Agna was no Viking, and the horde had chased after her when she went into the water.

Was the spirit lying?

There was no doubt Kole would see me dead, but he also needed my blade.

It mattered not. I would lure out the voldak and we would slay them all.

Vega slapped a hand on my shoulder and nodded.

Time to go.

Fey growled low and I patted his head. "Wait here."

The men spread out, and Flo handed me his torch. The light flashed across his bald head, shining on the black markings. Odin's Ravens. The same ravens tattooed on me. Odin would give us the strength, and if not, then his ravens would take us to him.

Firelight bounced against the stone wall of the cave. With light steps, I headed forward, eyes ahead, searching for the pool Kole had described. My thoughts went to Agna, and how I hoped the men back at the settlement were strong enough to defend any wandering voldak. It was the only reason we didn't bring more here.

Soft light waved in front of me. Squinting, I could make out the water of a large pool. Mist rose above the water and I placed the torch on the ground. I couldn't swim with my weapons or my shield, so I left them on the floor.

To the bottom and back up, as fast as I can.

While I couldn't see the bottom of the pool, the strange light gave enough light that I wouldn't be swimming in darkness. With one big breath, I dove into the water.

Warm.

My eyes adjusted to the water, and just like Agna said, far in the distance, that soft light brightened, and I could make out the shape of a massive structure.

No way we can swim that far. Agna was right.

I would find a way though.

Kicking my legs, I dove deeper, knowing I only had minutes before my breath would give out. Blackness covered the bottom. My heart raced. My chest tightened. I had to start swimming back up, but where was the horde? Why were they not here? Fire burned in my lungs so I swam to the surface, gasping as I breached.

Heaving, I pulled myself onto the cave floor.

"Grrr." I slammed the floor with my fist. Kole's *plan* didn't work.

There were no undead in the water, and if they were down there, they weren't coming up. I shook off the water, and quickly wrung out my clothes then grabbed my weapons and torch and headed back outside, aggravated. Where was Kole? I clenched my fists, ready to punch him in the throat.

The screams reached my ears before I even reached the woods. I ran, throwing the torch aside, gripping my axes in my hands.

Moonlight shone ahead. Under its gloom, voldak fought with my men. The horde was upon them. More than thirty. Vega and the two men we had rummaged up from the village were engulfed by a tide of terror and steel.

Flo and Caspian were closer to me, and had not yet been inundated by the wave of undead. Chanting with his holy symbol in hand, Caspian held out his cross and dumped a bag of salt in a circle around him. Upon finishing his hymn to the heavens, the salt burst into a bluish flame, rising to his chest.

"The flames won't burn the living, but shall keep the undead at bay," the priest yelled.

Flo tested the theory as he kept its deadly diameter to his left, forcing a bottleneck between it and a high mound of earth that supported a large pine tree to his right.

The group of undead that passed Vega and the other two men, cautiously approached Flo and the ring of fire. With a thunderous battle cry, Flo's blade ignited, passing through the ring of fire as it cut horizontal across the first two assailants.

Azure flames enveloped the creatures as the keen blade struck true.

Three more spun away from the outer ring of the menacing

loop of holy fire, only to be met with a flash of heat. Flames sprung out at them as Caspian, whipping a large vial of fluid, sent a spray of incendiary death in their direction.

"Greek fire, you godless beasts," Caspian yelled as the undead burned.

I charged headlong into the fire, having no time to doubt the priest's words. Wreathed in a lightning blue blaze, I burst through the wall of flames, axes slicing through the last two creatures of the frontal assault group, igniting their pale white flesh, which quickly turned black as they dissipated into ash.

Kole was nowhere to be seen and neither was Fey. Where could those two be?

Vega emerged from the fray, steel whirling around him at incredible speeds. Limbs showered the ground as he made his way out of the vicious mob. A score of wounds adorned his flesh, but he wasn't showing any signs of slowing. All of Valhalla must have watched in awe.

Heavy sweeps of his massive bastard sword cleaved through the undead ranks. Back peddling, he tried to make his way out of the horde. Unaware of the blade approaching his back.

"Vega, behind you," I yelled.

I wouldn't make it in time, and Vega couldn't hear my plea over the din of combat. Rushing with all my might, I winced as the death blow came at him.

Streaks of black and silver came out of the woods, across from one another and perfectly coordinated. Fey latched on to the voldak assassin's sword arm, at the elbow, spinning him and the weapon away from Vega's back.

The voldak's rotation brought him face to face with the open maws of the obsidian beast whose eyes burned with supernatural hate. Massive fangs clamped shut on the monster's face, its powerful jaws crushing bone as it tore the head free from the creature's neck.

Attackers closed in on Vega's flanks. A blade pierced through his left thigh and the enraged warrior grunted in pain. Grabbing the undead's wrist as it held the impaled blade, Vega pulled the creature into a pommel strike that caved its face in then released a devastating backhand slash that caught two more voldak on his right flank. The blade bit into the monster's flesh, flaccid torso splitting apart and showering the warrior in a rain of blood.

I was only ten feet from Vega when another voldak warrior struck at him from behind, taking his arm clean off. Vega's grip was so strong it still held the dead creature's wrist as the limb and its victim's carcass fell away.

"Valhalla!" Vega shouted, a death wail that rocked throughout the forest. Even the voldak flinched from its rage.

The word traveled through me igniting my own rage as I hit the pile, axes whipping and slashing in a hell bound fury.

I screamed Valhalla at the top of my lungs, matching Vega's intensity, letting my brother know I fought beside him as he met his death. I placed my back to his, supporting the fading warrior as he fought to stay conscious. Invigorating the dying warrior's spirit, Vega snapped back into his wits, reacting off pure anger. For the next minute, we became a flurry of death and destruction, hacking and weaving in and out of each other's attack. Steel ringing loudly in my ears as blood caked on my flesh. Blades nicked my skin, but nothing solid enough to slow my onslaught.

A cyclone of carnage, I hacked through their number. I was lost in a death frenzy, each dodge and strike moving on instinct. The blur of combat clouded out the worry and fear, nothing mattered but seeing every single voldak slaughtered.

A hand grabbed me by the collar, and the next thing I knew I was flying backwards out of the pile. Vega took multiple swords through his chest and abdomen, a few undoubtedly meant for me.

Blood seeped through his grinning face. He had found a glorious death which ensured his ride home.

Flo screamed, but a buzzing sounded in my ears. My gaze locked on Vega as his body sank below the mist and disappeared beneath the ranks of the undead warriors.

"Snap out of it, ye deaf manic!" Flo shook my shoulders, but I couldn't move my gaze from where Vega fell.

The horde surrounded us. We were dead men out of options.

I don't know if I can do this.

A wave of despair slammed against my chest, swirling with the rising fear that the second strongest man I knew just fell. How could I beat these monsters when Vega couldn't? I'm not stronger than him.

Kole appeared from behind us, a sword in each hand. One was broken and the size of a short sword, the other a thin, long sword, both impressive looking in comparison to his lithe frame.

"Have you left the rest for me to clean up?" A smile stretched across Kole's blood-stained face. Red covered everything under his eyes. His shaggy auburn hair danced wildly, while he slashed and darted in and out of the lethal melee. "You're better than I expected Folkvarr. I would have pegged you for death five minutes ago." Kole grinned back at me. "Now get off your ass and help me with these abominations, unless you're fine with them killing your friend."

"We need you lad! Your father needs you." Flo rose to his feet joining Kole. "Besides, we can't let him rob all the glory," Flo said motioning to Kole

Fey's fur brushed my arm, a loud growl to the side of my head, beckoning me to regain my spirit and fight. I gripped his fur for support, trying to find the strength to rejoin my brothers.

Vega's bloodied face flashed through my mind.

I cannot lose another brother. I won't.

Grasping my shoulder, Caspian helped me stand while chanting a blessing over me. His words strangely rung in my ear as he prayed to his foreign god. A calm washed over me as the hymn ended. Invigoration coursed in my veins. Power pulsed through my muscles as if a raging torrent had been released inside of me. A sensation of invincibility overflowed from my core.

Flo swung in complex slashing patterns, keeping many of the voldak at bay while Kole utilized his speed and accuracy to pick off targets rushing at the deadly duo.

The undead surrounded them like they had Vega. Heat built in my body, sending me into motion. I was moving much faster than I normally could. I went wide and right, running up a mound of uneven ground, on the horde's left flank, easily traversing the terrain in leaps and bounds. Nearing the precipice, I threw the axe in my left hand in a downward spin, aiming at the nearest voldak's head. Its edge buried deeply into the side of the unsuspecting creature's skull.

Leaping forward, I kneed the undead next to him directly in the spine, snapping vertebra. The voldak flew forward impaling its sword through the back of the undead in front of him. Crash landing, while swinging a horizontal chop to the creature on my right, I lopped off the upper part of his skull, cutting completely through its face with a diagonal slash.

Retrieving my axe, I pried it quickly from the wound. The rough patches of the voldak's hair were now slick with its own blood.

A combatant rushed in at my side, thinking I was open for its attack. Fey leapt in, shredding the voldak to pieces. His gray fur adorned with streaks of blood looked viciously fierce.

Four had fallen in a matter of seconds. Never had I felt so powerful and capable. My father's face flashed before my eyes. The thought of him being dead, or worse, turned into one of these abominations, sent a seething wave of aggression through me. I felt like an uncaged beast, and only their destruction would sate my hunger.

"Ahhhhhhhhhhhhhhhhh!" I screamed while Fey growled, louder than I had ever heard him.

The entire horde turned toward us. Our war cry so menacing that even in their blood-shot beady eyes, I could see a recognition of caution.

Kole didn't let the opportunity pass, dispatching two more creatures, back into the deep bosom of Hel.

I waded into the undead ranks, fear had long left me. Roaring while striking blow after blow, batting away their attacks and feeble attempts to parry my deadly dance.

I made it to Vega's body, a swath of destruction in my wake. Hunching forward, I swiveled back and forth between the nearest targets. Three rushed in, their mouths open in blood-curdling screams. They must have realized the shift in momentum and were willing to lose more to stop me. Bracing for the impact, I smiled at them.

Kole zipped past me, both swords pointing forward then fanning out after clearing my flank. Streaking into the gap between the right and middle voldak, Kole eviscerated the duo, slicing all the way through their bodies.

The third creature spun at the violent flash blurring past him, and I took my axe to his temple, dropping him instantly.

More than twenty were dead, but still not the whole lot. Men who were massive in life and even more imposing in death, made their way toward us. Luckily, they were moving slower than the ones we had already killed. Still, my muscles ached; the enchantment Caspian had placed on me quickly fading.

One of the undead fed on Belbog like he was a large wineskin, guzzling globs of blood from his lifeless body.

Flo, Kole, and Fey were at my sides, Vega's broken body before us. I was about to call for Caspian, when the uncanny priest made his way past me and Flo.

"Per virtutem sanguinis Iesu Christi et in Spiritu Sancto." Caspian chanted again in his language. He bent down and touched Vega's body with one hand then holding his arm outstretched, clutching the cross, he yelled, *"Ad Cinere!"*

White light coursed from under the earth and up through Vega's body. His eyes opened and fire erupted from within him. Out of the mist, a bright white apparition that resembled the proud warrior rose like a flame. Turning once to regard us, with a familiar grin on his face, the phantom of our fallen brother, spun back toward the enemy, dashing at them.

Fast as a bolt of lightning, he collided with the front of the horde, directly into the large one who was drinking from Belbog. Fiery gusts exploded upon impact, turning the front line into ashes where they stood.

"Even in death you are impressive brother!" Flo said, shouting praise to our fallen comrade.

"Next time start with that," Kole added, amazement in his eyes.

"I need the life force of one who has recently departed this realm," Caspian stoically replied.

"If that's the case, next time we can feed them Kole." I grinned at the spirit boy beside me.

"Last time I save your worthless hide," Kole grunted.

"Save it children, we are not yet done here." Flo readied his blade and focused on the remaining undead.

"Even though they are only seven, stay cautious." I didn't want to be overconfident. We were all tired, and running out of tricks.

"You mean six." Kole whipped his short sword with deadly accuracy, at one of the massive creature's heads. The blade moved with incredible speed as it wind-milled at the voldak's face, striking it between the eyes.

"Aye, six it is." Flo laughed and broke into a sprint.

"Show off," I said, shaking my head.

"Gentlemen," Caspian said alerting us to the four headed our way.

Fey hit one from the back, momentum taking him and the creature to the earth below. Fey's powerful jaws ripped the head off the creature's shoulders.

"Good, boy," Kole and I said at the same time.

I would have glanced at him, but a man bigger than my father, with half of his pale face burned, swung a halberd at my face

While I fought the monstrosity with the halberd, Flo struggled to make an offensive move with the one he'd decided to charge.

Two more came in at me swift and with accuracy. Parrying the first, I ducked the last strike, its deadly spear tip nicking me on the cheek, cutting a line under my right eye.

This isn't over yet.

"Help!" Caspian cried, but I was in no position to do so.

Luckily, Kole was quick enough to cross the gap and intercept a blade that would have surely felled the priest. However, this cost him a debt in blood as the beast he was fighting caught him with a slash across his back.

Caspian lay face down in the dirt and mist and couldn't see Kole's eyes, but I caught them for a fleeting moment. Burning embers glowed beneath his shaggy bangs, reminding me he was much more than a mortal.

"Enough with the games." Kole's voice deepened, a seething tone of rage.

A red glow emanated from Kole's body. His skin changed to black as the night sky. Blindingly quick, the boy thrust his arm through the undead swordsman's abdomen, his fist erupting out of the creature's back.

The sight was terrifying. The power he possessed beyond anything I had ever witnessed. So quickly had the attack taken place, by the time Caspian turned back around, Kole changed back to a normal boy.

I dodged the voldak with the halberd, only to be met with another long sweeping strike, this one higher and aiming to take my head. I spun under it, bending in a back bridge while chopping at the voldak's inner thigh with my main hand. The weapon cut within inches of my face, slicing one of the braids from my hair clean off.

I scored a hit, lacerating a slash across the monster's thigh. Continuing the momentum of the spinning back bridge, I came up and around in a complete pirouette, the mud beneath my heels helping me rotate. I was behind his weapon's momentum, quickly I bridged the gap sending the axe in my off hand into his gut, which lodged and got stuck. My right hand sent a vicious backhanded strike, slicing the creature's throat.

Its massive forearm struck me in the side of the head, shoving me to the ground. I went with it diving into a front roll. I spun as I came up and threw my remaining axe wildly at his face.

The beast charged with the halberd low, aiming to skewer me where I crouched. I don't know if it was luck or skill, maybe Vega's ghost was still affecting the field of combat, but my axe spun in a crescent curve, which came in at an angle and hit the creature behind its ear, killing him instantly. I dove out of the way, and the behemoth crashed where I was just crouching, mud and dirt flying into my face.

Turning onto my back, I saw Flo and Kole smiling above

me. "Caspian?" I was worried our priest didn't survive.

"He's fine, little brother," Flo said, helping me up from the mud. "You fought like a man possessed by Thor himself. Your Father would be proud." Flo clapped a hand on my shoulder.

"He did okay," Kole said from behind Flo, his eyes flashing a red-hot gleam for a brief second.

"Aye, the bards will sing of this day for years to come." Flo lifted his sword into the air.

"That's if we survive the rest of the night," the muddied priest said as he joined the group, glancing around at the woods.

The undead lay strewn all around us. In the end, more than sixty warriors littered the battlefield, and that's what we could tell from the ones who weren't incinerated by Caspian's spell. Vega, Belbog, and Belbog's man had fallen.

Fey howled at the moon.

"He would be proud indeed," Flo said, one last time as he patted me on the back.

My thoughts weighed heavily as I thought of my father. Soon I would learn of his fate and face what that truth meant.

22

Flo and I watched the fire burn away the dead. Vega had been with us since the beginning. We'd left home together, fought together. He died a warrior's death, and one I was glad to have witnessed.

"Odin will be at the gates waiting for him." Flo raised a horn and chugged the ale down.

"We need to get my father."

"Aye, we will."

With the horde gone, we had a straight path to the underground palace. Though none of us knew if more voldak were in the woods, or how fast they could be created. We had yet to discover the witch, and without her, the voldak could still come forth.

My thoughts switched to Agna. I wanted to make sure she was safe, but we couldn't risk any of the horde returning. Caspian offered to leave and check on her. I think the priest had seen enough blood and death to last him a lifetime. Surprisingly, he only vomited once when we were piling up the bodies to burn.

"You're thinking of her." Flo grinned.

His statement made my heart race.

"Don't deny it," he added. "And I don't blame you. She is very pretty."

"Careful, Flo."

He chugged the rest of the ale from his horn. "I don't care who you bed, but Holemgeiir will."

When he turned to face me with that wicked grin, a mixture of panic and anger swirled within me. "My father has no say in who I bed."

Flo slapped my shoulder and stared into my eyes. "Aye, but you don't want to just bed her, and you cannot marry a Slav."

He gave me no chance to refute and patted my shoulder before leaving me alone.

He was right.

I didn't just want to bed her.

Rain fell from the sky, smothering the pile of burning bodies into ash. It seemed even the gods wanted this blight off their lands. Knowing our job was done, I whistled for Fey, found Flo, and we ran back to the settlement.

Every muscle and joint screamed as I ran, yelling at me to rest, but my heart pumped me with speed. The urge to see Agna carried me through any physical fatigue and pain draining my limbs.

I had just broken past the tree line when Caspian ran toward me.

"What is it?" I yelled, not slowing. "What's happened?"

He stopped short and leaned over, catching his breath. "Agna and Danica were attacked."

Fear raged through me. "Where are they?"

"In the house." He pointed to Agna's home. The door lay splintered on the ground.

I ran to her home. My chest constricting with worry. *I shouldn't have left her.* "Agna!"

Screaming her name, I charged inside. She sat on the floor near a bed. She lifted her head. Bruises and blood caked her face and mouth. When our gazes met, she cried.

In a moment, I was at her side, pulling her into my arms. "You're safe now."

She sobbed and gripped my shirt. The pain in her voice rocked my core. I couldn't hold her any tighter. I sat on the floor, whispering words of comfort, stroking her hair, kissing every part of her broken face.

"Don't be afraid," I said softly. "I'm here. I'm here."

Holding her shaking body, I fought to find words of comfort. This whole time I was off fighting, she was here, fighting for her own life. The horror she must have endured . . . How could I say anything to quell that fear?

Her sister lay on the bed, pale, and sickly looking. Shallow breaths left her mouth.

What happened here? I wanted to ask, but Agna cried and burrowed her face deep into my chest, hiding from whatever horrors took place. It was then I noticed a body in the corner.

Slowly, I moved Agna to the side and behind me. "Agna, who is that?"

A blanket had been draped over the figure. The only telling features were the big hands and booted feet sticking out.

"My father," she cried. "He . . . he came back."

"But your father's been dead?"

She nodded, the tears streaming down her face.

"By the gods." I looked back at the body. "I have to get rid of it."

"I know." She turned her head, and leaned on the edge of the bed, closer to her sister.

Keeping the blanket on, I grabbed an arm and dragged the dead man outside. I needed a flame to burn the body, but not here.

Caspian walked over, his eyes going wide. "Is that what attacked them?"

"Yes, and we need to burn the body. Flo!" I shouted at Flo who was dunking his head in a nearby trough. "I need you!"

He shook the water off his face, and jogged to us. "What's this?"

"Undead," I said, dropping the body. "I need to make sure Agna isn't hurt. She's a bloody mess. Can you two handle this?"

Flo and Caspian nodded.

"Good." I wiped my hands and turned to go back inside.

"Folkvarr, wait." Caspian pulled me aside. "Her sister was bitten."

"Bitten? What does that mean?"

He wiped his forehead, smearing his already dirty face. "If a voldak bites you, you can turn into them or at least that's what the tales say. One of my brothers may have a cure."

I glanced in the home at Danica laying still on the bed, Agna in a crumpled heap next to her. "Go, rest. I'll stay here tonight."

He nodded, and I went back to Agna. Blood splattered her face and clothes. Her dress had a big rip, revealing scrapes across her back. Whatever happened here, had been horrible.

Gently, I took her hand and helped her stand. She grabbed my arm for support and winced with each step. I broke away to pick up the knocked over table and chairs and set them right.

"Sit," I said, and helped her to the chair.

While she sat, I searched for a pot of water and salves to help clean the wounds. A wooden bowl sat next to the fire. I sniffed, *clean*. I picked up the bowl and a rag and sat in the other chair.

"What happened?" I dabbed the rag in the water and gently rubbed the blood off her face.

She winced at my touch. "Our father returned. Danica couldn't believe he was anything other than our Papa, but he wasn't. I attacked him, but he was too strong and got to Danica. I barely saved her."

"But you did save her. She still lives."

Agna nodded. Her eyelids fluttered and her shoulders sank. When I had wiped all the blood off her forehead, I dragged the cloth to her cheek.

"Did you succeed?" she asked.

"We did. The horde is destroyed. We have a clean path to the palace."

"I'm glad."

I touched the rag to her bloodied lip. "Am I pressing too hard?"

"No."

Our gazes connected. I wanted to reassure her I would never leave her again. "I'm sorry I wasn't here. It won't happen again."

"You couldn't have known. I'm still not sure how it's even

possible he was here." Her green eyes glistened and a tear escaped.

Taking the rag, I slowly wiped the tears off her face. Everything in me wanted to hold her, and never release. She could have died tonight, and that single thought sent my mind into a frenzy. Taking a deep breath, I controlled the fear and anger rolling through me. I dotted her mouth with the rag, gently cleaning the blood off her lip.

Her lips brushed against my fingers. I traced her mouth with my thumb. Her breath was warm and I wanted to kiss her, but she was broken, emotionally and physically.

"What can I do?" Besides cleaning her, I didn't know what else to do. I would have to fix her door, clean up the broken wood, make sure her sister didn't turn and kill her.

"Will you stay?"

I cupped her face with my hands. "Of course, I'll stay. I'm not ever leaving you again."

She left her chair, and I slid back to let her sit on my lap. When she curled into me, my body heated with worry and sorrow. Tonight, death had come too close, for both of us. In that broken moment, I realized how much I cared for her, no, not cared, I *loved* her. A love so powerful, I didn't care what my father would say or her family, or anyone else who thought we shouldn't be together.

This precious, brave, beautiful girl had me wrapped in ways I couldn't explain or fight against. I wasn't going to leave her, and if that meant I had to stay here, in this tiny settlement, so be it.

23

Morning arrived and every muscle ached. Folkvarr snored in the chair, his head laying on his folded arms. He'd insisted on staying with me to stand guard, but he must have fallen asleep. I grabbed a blanket from my bed and laid it across his shoulders.

He breathed heavy and I leaned down to kiss his forehead.

Danica still slept. Sweat dotted her brow. I dipped a washcloth into the water bucket beside her bed and wiped her face. Purple bruising surrounded the bite mark on her neck. My heart lurched with fear.

I needed to go to Yaya. She would know what to do.

"Agna?"

Caspian stood by the door which hung slightly ajar. Folkvarr had placed it back in place as best he could and used our big tub to keep it shut for the night. I dropped the cloth in the bucket and pushed the tub out of the way. Caspian nodded a good morning and squeezed past the broken door.

The door Papa had pushed me through.

A chill shook through my body and I wanted so badly to forget last night. To forget that Papa, dead for three years, somehow came back as a voldak, and came back for us.

"How is she?" Caspian leaned over Danica and touched her forehead.

I moved to sit beside her and again used the cloth to wipe away the sweat painting her red face. "The same."

"I have not met anyone who has been bitten, but one of my brothers has. I'll return to Kiev, and be back with answers."

Sadness filled my limbs. Each time I dragged the cloth across her skin, the sadness grew, blossoming into a circle of pain ready to burst my chest open. "She has to be okay."

Caspian placed a hand on my shoulder. "Have faith. I will be back as quickly as I can."

Folkvarr yawned behind us. "You're leaving?"

"Yes. I may be able to find a cure for her. Give me two days."

When Caspian left, I returned to washing the hotness off my sister.

"She looks worse." Folkvarr stood beside me. "Has she woken at all?"

"No. She's the same. I need to go to Yaya and tell her what happened."

"I am already here, child."

"Yaya"! I jumped and ran to her arms. "What are you doing here? How did you know?"

She squeezed me tight. "I heard the screams of the undead last night. One had traveled to my door, but my dear Lew stopped the creature."

I peeked through the open door. Lew stood outside chewing

the grass. The tips of his horns coated in blood.

"Oh, my Danica!" Yaya released me and hurried to the bed. "What happened?"

Folkvarr moved to stand near me. While he didn't touch me, feeling his presence helped me re-tell the whole tale. When I got to the part of Papa attacking us, and throwing me, my voice cracked and Folkvarr grabbed my hand. Yaya listened, her eyes watering, until the tears fell. I had only seen Yaya cry once. The day my parents died.

"I should have been here," she said, wiping away her tears.

"No." Folkvarr squeezed my hand, and I didn't care what Yaya would think as I leaned into his side and let him hold me. "You were safer in your hut. Voldak are deadly, and if you were here, you may not have survived."

It was true. Yaya would have protected us, and Papa would have killed her just like he had tried to kill me.

I wanted to ask if she knew what would happen to Danica but seeing her so upset, terrified me that she already knew what was happening, and it was bad. Still, *I* needed to know.

"Yaya . . ." My voice cracked and if it wasn't for Folkvarr's strong arm holding me up, I would have crumbled at the question. "Do you know what happens when you are bitten? Will she be okay?"

Yaya shook her head. "She will turn."

"What?" My head spun, and my legs gave out.

"Whoa." Folkvarr grabbed my waist. "Steady."

"What do you mean?" My body shook, and my breaths came faster.

"Breathe, Agna." Folkvarr was the only thing holding me on my feet.

"She will be one of them. Of this, I am certain."

"No! No! You're wrong!" I pushed away from Folkvarr as anger replaced fear. "Caspian says there may be a cure. He's going to get help."

"My dear grandmother told me of this. It has happened before."

"No, I don't believe you. I won't!"

I ran out of the house, my body shaking, tears blurring my vision. I made it to the edge of the woods before I crumbled to my knees and fell forward, gripping the grass with my hands, crying uncontrollably and screaming at the mist.

I can't lose Danica. I can't lose my sister. Why? Why is this happening to me? What did my family do to deserve this? I can't take it anymore.

"Shhh." Folkvarr pulled me into his arms.

I dug into his shirt, burying myself into his chest, and drenching him with my tears.

He hugged me and rubbed my back. "If Caspian thinks there is a cure, there's still hope."

"I can't lose her too." Each sob ripped my heart apart, tearing away with what little I had managed to put back together after my parent's death.

Folkvarr caressed my hair. He stroked the long strands, his fingers brushing against my neck. "Whatever happens, I will be here with you. We will save them both."

I knew he talked of his father. "But how can you be sure?"

"Because I choose to believe in hope rather than live without it."

24

Orange light filtered through the thick trees sparkling the morning. Lew walked alongside me. Yaya insisted he go with me to the well. It had been two days since the night Papa attacked. Two long, painful days with no change in my sister.

Caspian promised he'd return today. Yaya insisted there was no cure, but I chose to have faith in our Christian friend. Though each passing moment, the fear of my sister's fate grew. I had to do something, anything, to keep my mind off Danica.

A branch snapped. I whirled around, swinging the bucket.

"Whoa!" Folkvarr jumped back.

"Oh! I'm sorry. Don't sneak up on me like that!" I huffed, catching my breath. "What are you doing here?"

The rays of dawn twinkled his blue eyes. He wore a cotton tunic that opened at the neck, revealing the black raven's head. I followed the black tattoo traveling down to his hand. An interlocking pattern of black and blue knots.

"I needed to see you."

In one quick move, he closed the space between us and crushed me with his lips. The bucket slipped out of my hand, tumbling to the ground. He dug his fingers into my waist, into my hair, grabbing me as if I would run.

But Folkvarr had embedded himself into my heart. I would never run from him.

As the sun warmed our faces, I let my fear and panic fade away. His soft, full lips danced across my skin. Every time his thumbs pressed deeper into my waist, my toes curled with anticipation. I focused on how his mouth moved with me, making me forget everything but him.

Like the mist wrapped around the earth, I wanted Folkvarr to wrap around me, to encase me in his very essence.

He kissed the soft spot on my neck that made the world fade away, and trailed his lips down and down. "Marry me," he whispered.

"What?" My heart thumped. Had I heard him wrong. Marriage?

He grazed my face with his mouth. "Marry me."

The smile breaking on my face couldn't be held back. "Are you serious?"

"I've never been surer of anything in my life." Moving his mouth to mine, he held my face with his hands. "Be my wife."

How could I stare into those stormy eyes and say no? How could I deny the thought of eternity with him filled me with tingling exhilaration? And with death haunting us at every turn, I wanted each moment of my life to be spent with him.

"What about my aunt's arrangements?"

"I don't care what your aunt said." He rubbed my cheeks

with his thumbs. "We'll marry in secret then she won't be able to marry you off. I won't let anyone take you. I swear it."

"Where would we go? Where would we live?" I wanted this to be true. I wanted to believe we could be together, regardless of who would stop us. My sister would never approve, nor my aunt, but Yaya? Yaya would support love.

"It doesn't matter," he said in a hushed voice. "We'll find our own way."

I believed him. "Yes."

He smiled and lifted me off the ground, swinging me, both of us laughing and dizzy with joy. When he placed me back on the grass, a deep hunger filled his gaze. The mist swirled around our feet, shading us from prying woodland creatures, and he grabbed me in a feverish kiss.

He would be my husband. It seemed crazy, impossible, but the intensity of our bond only seemed to be growing.

Something tugged on my dress. I glanced back at Lew nibbling on the back of my rubaKHa. "Shoo!" I leaned over and pushed on the large ram who weighed much more than he should.

Folkvarr ignored the ram and kept his mouth tightly against my skin.

Stupid ram!

With the back of my foot, I shoved Lew away. He snorted and yanked on my apron, forcing me to break away from Folkvarr.

"Lew!" I yelled and swatted the stubborn ram. When I turned back to Folkvarr, his brow furrowed as he stared out to the woods.

"What's wrong?" I took his hand in mine and squeezed.

"It's your father. Isn't it?"

He cupped his free hand on my cheek. "I just realized I asked you to marry me without ever telling you I loved you."

I smiled. "I love you, too."

He pulled me close to his face and touched his forehead against mine. "I can't stop thinking about you. Night. Day. You consume me." His voice deepened.

No boy had ever spoken to me like that. Passionate and hungry. I could hear his need for me.

"I haven't been able to stop thinking about you either." It was true, and yet, I worried what would become of us after he found his father. Even if we married, it wouldn't stop the hate on both our sides.

Lew tugged on my apron again and banged his horns against the bucket on the ground.

"I better get water or Lew is going to ruin this dress."

"Here, let me." Folkvarr picked up the bucket and went to the well. His forearm muscles flexed as he pulled the rope, dropping the bucket into the well, then back up.

Sitting on the ground, I picked at the grass while watching him. His hair curled right above his shoulders, tickling the raven on his neck.

I could spend forever with him.

"Here you two are." Kole appeared out of nowhere. Suddenly, I was grateful for Lew's interruption. Having Kole catch Folkvarr and me in a deep kiss would start an argument or worse.

"What do you want?" Folkvarr took the now full bucket off the pulley.

"There's movement at the palace."

"What?" I jumped to my feet.

"Undead?" Folkvarr rushed over, spilling almost all of the bucket.

"No, I don't think so." Kole scratched his head. "I've seen more creatures swimming around there. The rusalki have their own guards, and well, I think they know we're coming."

"We have to go," I said to Folkvarr. "Before they move your father."

He nodded. "When can we leave?"

"Now," Kole said.

"Come, Lew!" I grabbed a horn and tugged him forward. "You need to go back to Yaya."

The three of us rushed back to the settlement where I left Lew. The boys waited outside for me while I went to check on Danica. Yaya sat next to the bed singing an old hymn. I leaned over and kissed her cheek. Without breaking song, she patted my hand.

Listening to a tune I'd known since birth, I pulled out an old crate from under my bed. After Mama passed, I kept her clothes in here. Sometimes, I would pick them up and remember her laugh. Sometimes, I would cry. I ran my fingers across a folded pair of brown trousers and a red tunic.

They were Mama's.

She wore them whenever we needed to scorch the earth, to grow our crops. I slipped out of my rubaKIIa and into her clothes. The scratchy material rubbed against my skin. This was the first time I'd worn an outfit from the crate. Danica thought we should leave Mama's things alone—if she wasn't lying half dead, she would be giving me a stern talking to.

But I couldn't swim in a dress, and I wasn't going to be left behind. I had to keep my mind off my sister. If I focused on her terrifying state, the fear would trap me in this room.

"Yaya," I said, sliding the crate back under the bed. "I'm going to the river for a bit. Lew is outside."

"Be safe," she said in between songs.

I didn't have the heart to tell her the truth.

I walked back outside. "I'm coming with you," I said to them. While I may not be as good a fighter as the three surrounding me, I wasn't useless. Without a dress, I could at least swim and move quicker.

"No." Kole eyed my attire, a pair of loose trousers and a shirt slightly too small. "It's too dangerous."

"He's right," Folkvarr said.

"Did you forget how Holemgeiir was taken? The maiden song? You're all in danger. Their magic won't work on me."

"The girl has a point." Flo joined our group, twirling his sword around.

He was the last one I would expect to agree with me, but I was thankful for it. "See. Even Flo agrees with me. I'm going." I shoved past the two boys, ignoring the concerned glances they both gave me.

"Hey." Folkvarr stepped beside me. "Do you still have the dagger I gave you?"

I lifted my shirt to show him the leather holster. "Yes."

"You don't have to come," he whispered. "If anything happens to you . . ."

Kole brushed against my other side. "And what are you two whispering about?"

"Nothing," I said.

"I doubt it was nothing." Kole's eyes flared red, and Folkvarr growled at him.

I grabbed Kole's arm and pulled him away from Folkvarr before he threw one of his axes at him. "May we speak? Alone?"

"Of course, *krasavitza moya*."

"Go on ahead, we'll be right behind you," I said to Folkvarr who glared at Kole. "Please."

He nodded, and slid his twin axes back into their holders.

When Folkvarr was far enough away, I turned on Kole. "Why must you antagonize him at every moment?"

"Have you told the young lad about our deal?"

Glancing ahead at Folkvarr, I knew I could never tell him the truth. It hurt too much. And now that we were to wed, I was sure he would try to kill Kole. I couldn't chance Folkvarr getting hurt. "No."

"You will let him fall madly in love with you, only to break his heart."

"I wouldn't do that."

"Ahh, my beauty, you already have."

I gasped as Kole shifted into a bird and took flight, laughing into the sky.

My hands trembled at the truth of my situation. How could I wed Folkvarr with this secret between us? My heart hurt at the conversation I knew I must have, but not now.

"Everything all right?" Folkvarr placed a hand on my back.

I jumped, shocked he hadn't gone ahead with the others. Though I should have guessed he wouldn't get too far ahead.

"It will be," I said, and smiled.

He kissed my forehead. "Ignore the spirit. He's jealous."

If only Folkvarr knew the truth.

"Where did he go?" Folkvarr glanced around.

"Who knows," I said. "Let's go."

He stroked the side of my cheek with his thumb. "Are you sure you want to come?"

I nodded.

He grabbed my hand, and warmth spread through me.

With our hands linked, we walked silently to the cave leading to the rusalki palace. I wanted to let go once we were close, but Folkvarr squeezed my hand. Kole was already there talking to Flo. He stopped mid-sentence when he saw us holding hands.

Sweat slid down my neck. What would Kole do when he learned the truth? He never explained what our bargain entailed, only that I would live with him and serve him.

What happens when I wed Folkvarr? If I left with Folkvarr then I might be safe. Kole couldn't take what he couldn't find.

Folkvarr brought my hand to his lips. With his gazed fixated on Kole, he kissed my knuckles before finally letting me free. Kole's eyes flashed red, but so quickly, I don't think anyone else noticed.

"These will allow you to breathe while swimming." Kole opened a satchel, and his gaze went to me. "This isn't going to be pleasant."

He lifted a gigantic snail out of the bag. Gray and green swirled along the edges of the shell.

"What are we going to do with that?" I leaned over, trying to see if he held an empty shell.

"Watch." Kole brought the shell to his nose and mouth.

Nausea rolled in my stomach. *I don't think I want to see this.*

A slimy, gray snail slithered out and covered his mouth and nose. It latched onto his face, and sucked on it.

"Ewww!" I turned my head, and covered my mouth.

"We're going to breathe with that?" Flo's face paled with the same disgust I felt.

Kole used a finger and pried the snail off. It made a wet suction sound and bile rose up my throat.

"Don't worry." He grinned. "Snails don't bite."

"Don't bite! How are we supposed to breathe with that on our face? Is this a joke?" I stomped over to Kole who kept grinning. "Be serious. How are we getting down there?"

He bent over and pulled out another snail. "This one has a dash of pink on her shell. I thought you'd like it." He dropped the snail into my hand and I shivered.

"How does it work?" Folkvarr sounded too calm and completely fine with letting that slimy creature kiss his face.

"At least one of you is being practical." Kole handed a snail to Folkvarr. "These are special little suckers. When they cover your face, they excrete a special concoction that will release oxygen into your mouth. As long as these guys are on, you can breathe underwater."

Folkvarr turned the snail over in his hand, examining the shell. "Let's go."

Flo and I exchanged a horrified glance. My mouth watered and I gagged just thinking of that slimy thing wiggling on my face.

Kole grabbed the bag and slung it over his shoulder. He seemed too happy about this whole snail thing. I wondered if there was another, gentler, non-slimy way to breathe underwater.

While Folkvarr and Flo walked into the cave, I pulled on Kole's shirt. "Is this really the only way."

He leaned against my shoulder, throwing his arm around me. "Dear, *krasavitza moya*, you must know I would never want anything other than me touching that pretty mouth."

Heat burst through my face. I could feel the red blossoming on my cheeks. Nervously, I glanced ahead where Folkvarr chatted with Flo. He must've not heard anything. "You shouldn't speak to me that way."

I shoved Kole's arm off my shoulders, and he laughed.

"Enjoy the time you have left with him. It'll be over soon."

A painful reminder of the bargain I had struck. A stupid bargain, yet, here we were about to save Folkvarr's father. If I had to choose again, I would still make the same decision.

Following the bobbing orange light from Flo's torch, I knew I would have to find a way to break the bargain. I would have to tell Yaya what I did. She still didn't know the price for Kole's help or that her gem hadn't worked.

If I'd learned anything over these past weeks, it was that anything was possible, including breaking the bargain that tied me to Kole.

25

Remember to keep the snail on your face, and breathe through it." Kole put a hand on Agna's shoulder. "Usually, I'd let a lady go first, but it'll be best if you all follow me."

Kole winked and dove into the water. I doubted he even needed the snail to breathe. Something told me he didn't want Flo to know his true nature.

Flo slapped the snail onto his face and shivered. Rarely, have I ever seen him so distressed. He dropped the torch before diving in.

Agna held the snail in her hand, gawking at it.

"You don't have to do this. It's safer here." I rubbed the side of her arm.

"No," she said. "I'm coming. I just need a moment."

I kissed the top of her hair.

"Okay, deep breath." She squeezed her eyes closed and brought the snail to her face. When it started crawling out, she screeched and jumped on her toes.

"Relax," I said, rubbing her back.

She shook her head, continuing to keep her eyes shut. When the snail completely covered her mouth, I checked the sides to make sure it sealed to her face. The creature breathed up and down. Its two antennas wiggled.

"Can you breathe?" I asked.

Opening her eyes, she nodded.

"Let's go. I'm right behind you."

Holding the shell, she walked to the edge and jumped in the water. I took my snail and pushed it against my face. The wet slime slithered over my nose and mouth. First I thought I couldn't breathe, but instead of the snail being solid, its body was light. When I breathed in and out, air rushed into my lungs. The sides clamped shut around my nose and mouth, almost like the snail liked to be here.

Diving into the pool, I swam toward Agna. My eyes stung at the cloudy water. The light in the distance brightened, highlighting a tall spire of bone white. Red shapes darted around the outside, and instead of swimming closer, Agna shifted to the left, following the others. Kicking my feet, I swam faster, catching up. Kole dove to a bunch of rocks and stopped.

When we all arrived, Kole pointed to the red shapes swarming the tall white palace. None of us could speak, but I could tell by how fast those shapes moved, we weren't getting past them. He held out his palm and made a circle across it with his finger then pointed to the cavern ahead of us.

Going around.

Kole gave a thumbs up and we dove deeper, straight to the dark hole nestled into the rocks. I glanced behind us, expecting to see one of those red shapes head our way, but we were in the clear, for now.

The snail stuck on without the need for me to hold it in place, which made swimming easier. I wondered how Vega and Father would react to breathing underwater, a feat I never thought possible. Somewhere within that castle I knew Father lived. If he had fallen, Odin's ravens surely would've visited me by now.

Staying here with Agna meant never seeing my brothers again. As the oldest it was my duty to protect them, train them to fight and survive. When we left home, it was only temporary. A voyage across the sea to explore the Viking settlement of Novgorod. Once Father met Rurik and saw his vision for our future, we returned home and brought the rest of my family here.

If Father fell, I would be responsible for my family.

Don't think about it. He lives.

Strange yellow stones covered the bottom and sides of the rocky cave, giving off just a tiny bit of light to make our way through. Thick cords of green algae hung from above us, grazing the top of our heads as we passed. The cavern narrowed, and only Agna's curvy form swam in front of me.

Too bad she isn't in a dress.

Hungry thoughts filled me as I imagined her in a dress, the fabric swaying open in the water, revealing every precious piece of her. I could taste the honey of her lips. The sweet desire she caused from the slightest glance of those mesmerizing green eyes.

Agna slowed, and righted herself, treading in the water.

Her tunic floated, revealing her back. I slid behind her and grabbed her hips, grazing her waist with my fingers. With the snail plastered on my face, there'd be no kissing, but I could still touch her.

She kicked her legs, pushing against me. If we weren't so far from the surface, I'd take this blasted snail off.

Slowly, I trailed my hands up her sides, taking her all in, desperate to touch her skin.

She slapped my hands.

It wasn't until a snake snapped at her head that I realized what was happening. Its fangs missed her face and she quickly pulled us both to the side. I grabbed my axe and swung, but the snake quickly swam upward, disappearing into a dark hole in the rock. Agna held out her dagger. Both of us watched the water, waiting.

The snake shot out from above. I shoved Agna aside, ready to slice the creature's head. Its thick body twisted around in the water, shifting angles, quickly. Agna lashed out at the tail with her dagger, slicing the side of the creature.

Its yellow-slit gaze turned on her. Quicker than I anticipated, the snake coiled around Agna. I took out my second axe and threw my whole body into the attack. The snake dodged left, dragging Agna with it. She stopped hacking at the snake to hold the snail to her face, her eyes wide.

Oh no. Fear and panic beat against my chest. If the snail sensed the danger, it may pull out and leave, then no matter how quickly I killed the snake, Agna would run out of air and drown.

A sword sliced through the air, lopping the snake's head off. The head floated up to the ceiling of the cavern. I sheathed my axes, grabbed the body and unfurled it from Agna.

Flo patted my shoulder before swimming back to where Kole treaded water. Spirit boy glared at me, and it was the first time I deserved it.

Are you okay? I cupped Agna's face with my hands, asking the question with my eyes. She clapped her shaking hand over mine and nodded.

We fell back in line, slowly winding our way through the narrow stretch. Silver fish darted by in schools, and an old, gigantic turtle nearly stopped our trek by deciding to squeeze past us.

Down and down we swam until Kole stopped.

With only the tiniest specks of light, it was impossible to know exactly where we were. It was like swimming in a clouded bath. He held up his hand, ordering us to wait while he swam upward.

The three of us treaded water. Strange hums and vibrations echoed through the water. We were far from where we first entered, the only exit I had seen. If we had to leave in a hurry, we'd have to swim hard and fast.

Did Kole bring a snail for my father? I'd been so eager to get here, I forgot to ask.

Kole came back and waved us forward. We swam up into a bright light. Breaching the water, we entered a rocky alcove, and there was air.

I yanked the snail off my face, coughing and spitting out the slime coating my mouth and throat. Flo vomited. Agna's face paled.

"Please, tell me we can leave a different way." Agna

shivered and dropped the snail beside her. It slithered a step or two before stopping then disappearing back into its shell.

"Depends," Kole said, picking up the snail and dropping it into a satchel. "There should be a land entrance, for when the rusalki don't want to drown their victims. But I'm not sure where."

When the coughing stopped, I lifted my head and froze.

Blood and black liquid splattered the walls and floor. To my left lay a giant insect leg, to my right, the head of a spider too big to be real. Broken cobwebs dangled in the corners of the room. One large web laid to the right with a half-eaten cocoon in the center.

"Whoa." I scurried back, shocked at what we were sitting in. "What is this?"

Agna screeched and jumped to her feet. "Is that a spider?"

"Was." Kole grinned as he collected the other two snails. "Spider guards. I had to come clean house. Easier that way."

I thought back to the battle of the undead. Kole had morphed into a spirit of pure night and fire. Not even Agna knew the power spirit boy held. It would take some serious skill to kill that one.

"I hate spiders." Flo threw the leg he had picked up, across the room.

"What do we do?" Agna was the first to ask Kole.

He glanced back and forth between us, and I wondered if the damn spirit even had a plan. He bent down and using his finger, drew a layout in the ground. "The palace is a spiral with rooms and corridors branching off from the center. Some angle down, others up to the surface. If your father is alive, he'll be in their cages. Here." He pointed to the bottom of the map. "You and Agna will get him and come back to the center. Flo and I will make sure the inhabitants are busy elsewhere."

Kole handed Flo and me small balls of cotton. "For your ears." He tapped his ear. "Keep it in."

I shoved the cotton inside my ear until the world around me muffled. Agna touched my side. If those cursed maidens somehow got through this measly barrier of fabric, she'd be our only hope. Suddenly, I was grateful to have her here.

Kole motioned us to follow. I gripped the hilts of my axes, cautiously watching the shadows for any signs of monsters or golden-haired witches. Sweat coated my palms, making my grip slip. The gray stone gave way to a sparkling coral floor. Smooth iridescent walls curved around us. Twinkling lights cascaded in bunches from the ceiling. The corridor curved around and around, leading upward, until it ended at a bone white door.

With a finger to his lips, Kole leaned his ear against the door. After two slow moments, he turned the handle and opened it.

Light sparkled off the shimmering pink crystal walls and the floor swirled a cloudy blue. My heart beat against my chest and drummed in my ears.

We were too open in this dome-shaped room, which was completely bare, except for a giant shell twisting from the floor to the ceiling. Six bone white doors circled the room. I prayed to the gods Kole knew which ones to take. The thought of being trapped in this palace, under the water, with no means of escape terrified me more than I would admit out loud.

Kole handed me his satchel. "In case we get separated," he

whispered. "Remember how we came in. When you hear an explosion, run back here, don't delay."

I nodded and slung the satchel over my shoulder.

He moved to Agna and touched her face. "Stay safe, *krasavitza moya.*"

Their gazes lingered too long on each other, and while I would normally threaten the spirit, he had been nothing but an ally. I let the offense slip, for now.

"You two go through that far left door," Kole said. "There's a room where they hold the males they keep alive. Be quick and quiet. Flo and I will be your distraction while I search for the other exit."

Flo flicked me a wave before trailing after Kole.

Agna tugged on my shirt, dragging me to the door. She released her hold on me to grab the twisted golden knob of the door. With both hands, she glanced back at me and I got my axes ready.

Ready.

Blue and white light poured out from the open door. The iridescent walls were replaced with a clear crystal that revealed the river on each side. Schools of black and silver fish zigzagged around the bright green algae that swayed from an edge of the outside walls. A deep moan sounded from the surrounding water, animal like. I couldn't imagine what type of beast it came from. One I didn't want to meet.

Moving in front of Agna, I gripped the hilts of my axes tight, waiting for something to crash through the wall, or screech out from the shadows blinking in and out around us. The corridor twisted, giving me no time to check for enemies. There were no places to take cover or hide behind if one approached. The thought of the water seeping in and being stuck down here, plagued me to the point of panic. The air tasted like wet earth and salt. What if Kole didn't find the other exit? I refused to let my father die down here. I'd give him my snail and let him and Agna go to the surface, though I doubted she would leave my side.

Stubborn just like Yaya's ram.

I glanced behind me to see how she was faring. She held her dagger in her right hand, her face strained with determination and those green eyes wide and bright.

We took the corridor down another level then another. It never opened to any other doors or exits. One long spiraling road, leading to death. When it finally ended, we stood in a round stone room with one massive golden door.

Would my father be on the other side?

Or was it a trap?

No, while Kole may have wanted me dead at first sight, he had an annoying interest in Agna. He would never send her to danger.

May the gods watch over us.

I pushed open the door, and there in a golden cage like a prized pet, lay my father.

"Father!"

He sprung to his feet, eyes wide. "Folkvarr? But how?"

I rushed at the cage, putting my weapons away, and pulled on the bars. "Where is the door?"

The cage was the size of a tiny room. Big enough for him to stand and walk around, with a bed and wash pan.

"They use magic," he said, moving to where I stood. "There is no lock, no latch. I've spent days searching." His voice mumbled through the cotton in my ears.

"There must be a way to break it." I pulled out my axes and slammed them against the cage. They clanged off the bars. The metal vibrated in my hands. I took the cotton out of my ears and shoved it in my pocket. "Open!" I slammed the bars with my body.

"Folkvarr." Father reached through the bars and placed a hand on my shoulder. He squeezed, forcing me to look at him.

"I will free you," I said, through gritted teeth. "I swear it."

"No, you must do something else."

Wailing echoed from down the hall. Agna ran to the entrance. She peeked around the corner and whispered, "I can't see anything yet."

"There is a witch they call Baba Yagga," Father continued, rushing the words. "She is leading the charge against our kind. Find and kill her or our brethren will never be safe."

"The only thing I'm doing is getting you out of here." My father was a fool if he thought I would leave him.

He grabbed my wrist. "Listen, boy. I have seen men come and go, broken until the sirens have had their fill then left to the waters where they return undead. You cannot allow this atrocity to stand anymore. The maidens answer to the witches."

I fought the anger boiling within my chest, begging me to yell and break the cage with my hands. "If you're asking me to abandon you, I can't."

"I ask that you obey your father." He tightened his hold on my arm. "Stop the witches, or these waters will never be safe for us. Think of how many of our brethren would fall to this fate. To never see the halls of Valhalla."

Gripping his arm, I held on to the last moment we might share. "How am I supposed to walk away and leave you to these monsters? How can I fight without you?"

"You are a Viking, and you will fight until you can't."

If only he knew about the others. How close I almost came to death. How Vega rose up from his body saving us with the last of his spirit. There was so much I wanted to say to my father, and I had no time.

Even caged, Father held his chin high, never showing defeat. Fighting until the very end.

"I'm going to find a way to break this cage, or I'll take the whole damn thing out of the palace."

Father laughed and pulled me closer until our heads touched the bars. "That's the Folkvarr I know." He kissed my forehead. "Go, and may Odin guide your axe."

Fear and sadness beat my chest, but I held all the emotion in. I would not break in front of my father. He needed to see my strength, to know that nothing would stop me.

The wailing from before, sounded closer.

"Folkvarr," Agna hissed as she ran back to me. "Something's coming."

"Go, now." Father released me. His eyes shone with the same sadness coursing through my body.

It nearly crushed my soul to leave him there. How could I abandon my father? How could I return to my family and face them with this news? I came all this way, just to fail.

Wails sounded from behind the walls, rising in pitch and

stirring the anger already building within me. Rage thumped inside my veins, evaporating the heartache into a tumult of fury.

I'd use it on them.

"I will find a way to save you," I said, tearing myself away.

"I know."

Agna and I dashed out the door. A *boom* shook the palace. I wobbled on my feet. "Are you all right?"

Agna blinked her eyes and rubbed her head. "What was that?"

"Our signal. We need to hurry."

Two rusalka rounded the corner. I shoved the cotton back into my ears, blocking their deadly calls before they seduced me into a stupor. Agna held out her dagger. With the maidens' voices dulled in my head, there was no stopping my charge. In one swift throw, I whirled my axes into their heads, dropping them to the ground. Grabbing my axes, we headed back to the main chamber to search for the rest of our party.

Where are they are?

Dozens of gray shapes slithered from the four other entranceways into the chamber. Slimy, fanged creatures, something between the large eels in the rivers and a lizard.

I grabbed Agna and shoved her behind me.

"There's too many," she said, holding out her dagger which would do nothing against the mass of creatures surrounding us.

"I'll cut a way to one of the exits. Stay close."

Swirling my axes, I slashed through the eels in front of me, only to be replaced by five more behind them. Agna screeched behind me, kicking and slicing at any that came too close.

"Need some help?" Kole grinned. I would almost be thankful for his timing if he didn't have a rusalka with him.

"What is this?" I yelled, turning my rage on to him.

His black eyes flashed red. "Fight first then I'll explain."

The maiden rubbed her bloody wrists, and avoided my glare. She cowered behind Kole, shivering in her thin silver gown.

Agna opened her mouth, most likely to yell at him, but quickly stopped when Kole began to disappear. His body widened, skin shifting brown and hairy, large tusks emerging from his mouth until he became a wild boar.

He charged at the creatures, shredding them and tossing them with his massive tusks. I followed his lead and sliced at the slithering lizards. Agna chirped behind me when one wrapped around her leg, but before I could reach her, she snatched the eel's head and chopped it off then tossed the whole oozy mess to the side.

"Where's Flo?" Agna called after jabbing at two more of the slimy creatures.

At the mention of his name, Flo walked in carrying the head of one of the maidens. "Taking my trophy. Did you find Holemgeiir?"

"Yes, but the cage he's in is held by magic. I can't open it." I glared at Kole on the last part, eyeing him to see if he knew it was impossible to free my father.

He snorted, never breaking away from my stare as he slaughtered the remaining lizards.

"Father gave me a lead on how to stop the undead and find the witch." I slid my axes back into their holders and surveyed the room. Black liquid splattered everything. The strange lizards twitched on the floor like fish on land.

"Then we find the witch," Flo replied, flinging the maiden's head over his shoulder like a satchel. "Suppose your friend here might know."

Kole shifted back into a human, his bare chest covered in black. "We ran into a situation. It was either shapeshift into a raven and open the lock or be eaten by a really hungry clam."

"What?" Agna and I looked at each other, asking at the same time.

A slapping sound came from the outer room. "We need to return to the surface, quickly." Kole touched the maiden's side. "Will you show us the surface exit?"

"Wait!" I grabbed Kole's arm.

The fire in his coal eyes flared, but I needed to know the truth. "My father is down there in a cage I can't open. If you know this place, you must know how to open it."

"What color was the cage?"

"Gold." The moment I said the word, the fire in Kole's eyes dimmed.

"There is only one gold cage in the palace. It is where the rusalki hold a prisoner of the witches. Not even I have the power to break the lock."

Rage turned everything in my mind into a haze. "You must've know this was a lost cause, so why bring us all here? Do you wish us all dead?"

Kole's gaze drifted too Agna. "It was a possibility, but no, I did not know. I fulfilled my bargain. That is all I'm required to do."

Agna gasped.

Dropping Kole's arm, I turned around to her. "You said

you made a bargain. What was the agreement? Was killing me part of it?"

Agna shook her head. "How could you say that? I told you it was to take us to the rusalki palace." Her face flushed. "Folkvarr, please."

"Whatever is going on with the three of you, do it on the surface." Flo pulled me away from Agna. "Not the time, boy."

"Let's go, then." I wasn't getting anymore answers down here.

Kole slid his arm around the maiden's waist and whispered into her ear. She nodded at his words, leaning against him for support. Her limbs trembled with each step.

The girl's eyes were so pale blue I wondered if her heart was frozen. Her white hair different than the others. There was no golden hue, and she didn't carry that same hypnotizing aura the others did. It was as if life had drained out of her.

We followed her to a far door, and up another twisting hallway, covered in the same clear crystal. It winded up and up, twisting and rising. I thought we would've already had to reach the surface by how high we traveled.

Blood trickled on the floor from the head slung across Flo's shoulder.

"Do you really need to carry that?" I jumped out of the way as another splash of blood almost hit my shirt.

"I'm going to pike it right outside and remind those wenches what happens when they leave the water." He gave me a wide, crazy smile.

We stopped in front of a white door with no handle. "Cover your ears," the maiden said.

She sang and a golden light traveled around the edge of the door unsealing whatever magic locked it. She pressed against it and it swung open, right into beautiful glorious day.

Thank the gods. I knelt on the ground and dug my hand into the dirt, never so thankful to have the earth under my feet.

"I'm going to look for a stick. Don't touch my head." Flo dropped the head on the ground, and I shoved it away with my boot.

"Really, Flo. It's disgusting. Must you keep it near us?" Agna covered her nose and mouth. "I'm going to be sick."

"Where can I find this witch?" I had no time to waste. The longer my father stayed prisoner, the harder it would be to set him free.

"We can discuss it when I get back." Kole whispered to the pale girl clinging to him.

"Get back?" I stood. "I need to find Babba Yagga now! What are you doing with this rusalka?"

Kole wrapped his arm around the girl's waist. "I need to take her to safety before the other maiden's come hunting."

"Why?" Agna stepped around me. "The rusalki work with the voldak. How can you be helping them?"

"Jealous?" Kole grinned.

"*Otstan' uzhe!*" Agna stomped her foot and Kole laughed.

I had no idea what Agna said, but by his reaction, I'm sure it wasn't a nice word.

"Don't worry, *krasavitza moya*. I'll return soon. You're not the only beauty who needs my help." He winked before shifting into the black wolf.

The pale girl stared at us, her too pale eyes making me shiver.

"Baba Yagga is not one," the girl said in a soft voice. "She is three, yet one is the head. Kill the head, kill them all."

Agna and I exchanged a confused glance. When I looked back at the girl, she and Kole were gone.

"Three?" I moaned. "How am I supposed to find three witches? What if Kole doesn't come back for days? I can't wait that long."

"We'll find them together." Agna slipped her hand through mine. "Kole will return." She said it with such certainty.

"How can you be so sure?"

Her gaze drifted to the treetops. "Because he must."

There was a strained tone in the way she spoke, and I didn't like it. Spirit boy made little sense, but he had been true to his word so far. If he said he would return, he would. Though, if his "bargain" was complete, what reason did he have for staying? The voldak threatened life. Maybe that was enough.

"I'm sorry about before." I pulled her closer. "You've done everything to help me." I lifted her chin with my finger, gently brushing her skin.

She looked at me with her entire soul and said, "I'm with you all of the way."

I hugged her, kissing the top of her head. "Thank you."

"Ahh!!" Agna jumped and closed my neck in a choke hold.

"What is it?" I lifted her off the ground, quickly scanning the woods for the threats.

"The head! Something is dragging it!" She squealed at the mess of blonde hair moving on the ground.

Whatever creature had it, suddenly darted off into the woods, taking the head with it.

"We better go after it." I unhooked Agna from my neck.

"You're joking."

"No, Flo will be really angry if we let his head get away."

"I am not chasing after a head!"

I grabbed her hand, holding in the laughter. "Oh, my dear, but you are." I tugged her squealing and yelling at me in her native tongue while we searched for a bloody head.

26

By the time we found the head—which had been taken by a fox—returned to Flo, and headed back to the settlement, the sky cascaded a beautiful orange and pink. I wanted to check on my sister and sleep. The day had been long, and I hoped she was faring better. I prayed to Perun Caspian had returned with answers.

My bones ached and a chill ran through me. Folkvarr wrapped an arm around my waist.

"Are you all right?" he whispered, his breath warm and melting the coldness on my neck.

"Tired, cold."

We stood outside the door to my home. The desire to soak in the warm tub, versus staying within Folkvarr's arms warred inside me. I turned into his comforting embrace, allowing his thick chest and strong arms to soothe away the day's events. "I'm sorry about your father."

"I'll free him. He won't die in that place."

"I know."

Folkvarr pressed against me. Clouds blocked the dying sun. In the shadows beside my home, he kissed me softly, sending my body into a state of relaxation. When he first arrived, I was angry at what his kind had done to my family, but now I knew he was not part of that same hatred. I would not blame Folkvarr for someone else's wrongdoings.

I pulled away, but he pushed forward, refusing to let me leave. His kiss washed over me, a fury of hunger and emotion. The desire to ease his pain, collided in a moment of passionate release. Our breaths beat against one another, driving away the cold. He needed to forget, and I desperately wanted to be the escape.

But my sister lay inside, wounded and hurt, and I needed rest.

With the lightest touch, I pressed my hands against his chest and gently pulled away. "If I could spend all night kissing you, I would, but I must check on Danica."

He sighed. His breath blew against my lips, and he nodded. "I will see you in the morning."

He turned and walked away. Suddenly, the cold left by his separation sent me into a strange panic. My heart thumped wildly, and I ran after him. "Wait!"

Before he fully turned around, I jumped into his arms, throwing mine around his neck. He lifted me off the ground as if I weighed nothing more than wisp of wind. I had never loved a boy before, never even kissed one boy, and now the thought of Folkvarr anywhere else but by my side caused me such pain.

"What is it?" he whispered, stroking my back as he held me.

"I don't know. It's hard to find the words, but even though I know I must go, I can't." The closer we came to solving all our problems, the more I worried what happened after.

He hugged me tighter then slowly lowered me to the ground. "I feel the same."

Too afraid to meet his stormy gaze and ruin this moment, I stared at the black tattoo rising up his neck.

He grabbed my wrists and touched his head to mine. "You have my heart, and I will never leave your side."

I relished those words, though the fear of Kole's bargain banged against my heart. "And you have mine."

He smiled, and kissed me again and again, until I finally had to catch my breath and say goodnight.

"I'll be by in the morning," he said, holding my hand, even as the distance between us grew.

Still smiling, I swung our linked arms back and forth. "I expect you at dawn, no later."

He winked, and I almost caved at his smile. "As you command."

We broke apart, and I went inside, closing the door behind me and leaning against it. Closing my eyes, I could still imagine his words and kiss, and how each one felt on my skin.

Danica lay on the bed, her face a sickly white. Sweat slicked back the edges of her hair which hung loose around her. Caspian should've returned tonight. What was taking so long?

Some cool water might help. Grabbing a ladle, I scooped up water from the small barrel and dumped it into a bowl then sat on the chair beside her bed. I took a rag, dipped it into the water, and washed the sides of her face and forehead.

Thunder boomed outside. Lighting flashed through the cracks in our home followed by a downpour of rain.

"I know you will pull through." My sister was strong and resilient. Even after the death of our parents, she did her best to continue with our normal daily routine. I dipped the rag again and washed behind her ear.

What is that? A black mark hid in the crook of her ear. Leaning closer, I used the rag to push away her hair and better see.

The bowl slipped out of my hands and crashed on the floor. *It can't be.*

My heart raced so fast my hands trembled.

Danica bore the witch's mark.

I dashed out the door and ran toward Juri's home and slid to a halting stop before cresting the hill. I couldn't go to Folkvarr. Regardless of how much he loved me, Danica was responsible for the undead and possibly his father being taken.

There was only one person I could trust.

Running as fast as I could, I headed to Yaya's. Once her tiny cottage came into view, I screamed out for her. "Yaya!" Panic scraped my throat and every part of my body trembled.

Yaya opened her door just as I crashed into her.

"What's wrong, dear? Come in." Glancing around, she wrapped an arm around my shoulders and pulled me inside. "I was just going to come back. I needed more herbs."

"Danica's the witch," I said, panting. I crouched over, holding my stomach and trying not to vomit from the run and fear. Every limb shook.

What am I going to do?

What is Folkvarr going to do?

"How can this be?" Yaya gripped my shaking hands. "Are you certain?"

"I was washing her face and found the mark behind her ear."

I wanted to vomit. My sister was the witch. How could she? Why?

"And you're sure it's the mark you saw."

There was no mistaking the star like figure Folkvarr and I saw on the forest floor. I nodded, unable to find the words to speak.

"We must hurry," Yaya said and pulled me outside into the wicked storm. "Before anyone finds out."

"What are we going to do? We can't protect her from the Vikings? She's not even awake," I yelled through the thunder, trying to shield my face from the rain.

"I will handle this." Yaya's stern voice kept me grounded. Her eyes did not waver for a moment. If anyone could protect Danica, it was her. "Help me bring her here, where I can keep her safe. The Vikings only need answers. If we get them, they'll have no need to harm her."

My hands shook. In one night, everything had changed. How could I lie to Folkvarr after we agreed to wed? I prayed to Perun he would understand, because I didn't know how to explain this.

"How will we bring her here?" I asked, but already knew the answer as Yaya unhooked Lew's gate and urged the ram forward. It wouldn't be a comfortable ride, but Lew would be able to carry Danica.

The night hid our presence as we raced back to the settlement. Mud covered my feet, and I stumbled more than once. My mind whirred with worry. What if we were caught? How would we explain moving Danica in such a state? Sweat coated my neck, my palms, drowning me in a sea of panic. What would I say to Folkvarr if he approached?

How could I lie to him?

But if I didn't . . .

No, he wouldn't kill my sister. I had to believe that.

The closer we came to our little home, the more I wanted to flee to the safety of the woods. How could Danica be the witch? Where could she learn such dark magic? Yaya had her tricks and herbs, but I had never seen her perform a ritual, and by the hard line creasing Yaya's forehead, I knew with certainty, she did not teach Danica these things.

"Stay." Yaya pointed at Lew and he waddled over to nibble on nearby grass.

With shaking hands, I peeked around the side of our home, searching the night for anyone out. Nothing. Slowly, quietly, Yaya and I walked into the house. Danica lay in the same spot, pale, and looking so weak my heart shattered. My little sister . . . *why*?

Yaya nudged my side. I walked over to the bed, my whole body shaking. I slipped my hands under Danica's arms and I lifted her while Yaya grabbed her legs. With urgent steps we rushed out the door and behind the house where Lew waited. I lifted Danica on top of Lew's back, wrapped her arms around his neck, and pushed him forward. "Go," I hissed.

Yaya watched behind us and I kept a hand on Danica's back, making sure she did not slip. The branches crunching under our feet sounded like an alarm that would wake anyone nearby. I cursed when I stubbed my foot on a rock.

The pain shot up my leg.

"It's terrible weather for a stroll."

Kole magically appeared in front of us, leaning against a tree, a lazy grin on his face, his arms casually folded over one another. The rain plastered his hair to his face

"Going to Yaya's." I met his coal-fire gaze, lifting my chin and showing no fear, though my heart beat against my chest like a drum.

"With your sister in her condition, during this?" He flicked a finger to the sky. "And riding a ram? Seems peculiar."

"If you have no business with us," Yaya said, "be gone."

Kole grinned and pushed off the tree. "Oh, Yaya, such a fiery soul."

Did Yaya know that Kole was a leshii? She pursed her lips and crinkled her nose at him.

"Move aside spirit." Yaya glared at Kole.

He narrowed his brow, and took a step back.

Did he fear Yaya?

"We have no time for games," she said. "My granddaughter is very ill."

"I see. Since I'm feeling generous, I'll help escort her back. Wouldn't want Lew to run off and poor Danica to fall."

I glanced at Yaya and she nodded. "Very well."

Kole slipped his hands around Danica, and jerked back, hissing as if she burned. "What is this?" He whirled around at me, the fire in his eyes coming to life.

"What . . . what do you mean?" I stammered, unsure of why he glared at me with such intensity.

"Black magic runs through her." His nose crinkled and the

fire in his eyes flashed brighter.

"She was bitten by a voldak," Yaya said.

"That is not from an undead bite." He stepped forward, keeping my gaze locked with his. "That is dark magic. Magic only the coven of Jezibaba uses."

Yaya gasped and clenched the fabric near her chest. "Do not speak that name. No one speaks that name." Yaya's voice trembled.

My body shivered, my clothes stuck to my skin. I stepped toward Kole, demanding answers. "Who are the Jezibaba?"

"Don't speak of them!" Yaya hissed. I barely heard her over the thunder, but the fear in her voice made my stomach clench.

"Kole?" The shaking attacked every one of my limbs and my mind raced for memories, or tales of the coven of Jezibaba, but I had never heard of them.

"She is the witch," Kole stated, and the fire in his eyes dimmed. "I am sorry, but your sister's fate is sealed. She is part of the coven now, and you cannot save her."

"I don't understand." One by one the tears fell. "What does that mean? Why didn't you say anything before? Folkvarr mentioned Baba Yaga and you said nothing!"

"I never trust a Viking," he said. "I was planning on doing a bit of research. It's actually why I'm out tonight."

"But Folkvarr has done nothing, but be honest."

"Yes. Folkvarr is *different*." He sighed and ran a hand through his hair. "Poor, Agna. What will your Viking lover say when he discovers your sister is the witch?"

"Please," I said, holding my hands to my lips in a prayer. "We will find a way to save her. Once she's well—"

"He'll kill her if he knows the truth."

Tears slipped down my cheeks, blending with the raindrops. No, he wouldn't. He *couldn't*.

"I loathe the coven," Kole said, eyeing Danica's limp form. "Their tainted spells and curses." He spat at the ground. "But I hate Vikings more, and so, I will keep your secret and help you anyway I can."

I released the breath I had been holding, and wiped my face with my hands.

"But know this, *krasavitza moya*, if your sister is in league with the coven, sharing their secrets will mean her death."

Before I could ask more, he shifted into a raven and disappeared into the night.

"Ignore the leshii," Yaya said, pushing Lew to continue. "They're not always right."

No, but this time I believed his every word.

27

Before the rays of dawn fully peeked over the sleeping lands, I left the longhouse, eager to see Agna. The night before had left a warm mark on my heart. She was fragile, yet strong, and nothing like the stories of Slavs I had come to know. My place was not among her people, or her lands, but I would risk the gods' wrath if it meant I could spend eternity holding her in my arms.

Fey yawned from outside the longhouse, licking blood off his front paw. I knelt beside him and scratched behind his ear.

"Already eaten, have you?"

He rubbed against my hand and I scratched harder. Memories of my first encounter with the wolf brought me back to that time long ago.

At the age of thirteen, I had killed a dire wolf, a rite of passage by my people. While skinning the beast later, I'd heard small whines coming from the bush. Fey, only a youngling then, had followed his dead mother to my camp. I decided to keep the pup, unsure if the wolf would turn on me or not. Five years later and he had become a trusted companion, and one who had saved my life more than once.

Giving him one last scratch, I stood and jogged to the thatched home at the far end of the village. With most of the people sleeping, I quietly knocked on Agna's door with my knuckle.

A minute or two passed, and she didn't come.

I leaned against the door, placing my ear on the wood, and listened for movement. Silence.

Too silent.

Risking her wrath at being woken or catching either of the girls in an indecent manner, I pushed the door open.

"Agna?" I spoke to an empty room. The chair by the bed had been knocked on its side. I walked over to the fire pit and slowly stuck my hand into the ash.

Cold. They left long ago, but where to?

I replayed last night's kiss with Agna. She had seemed happy, but Danica was still sick. She wouldn't risk moving her sister, not in that condition, which meant something had happened to them.

Fearful someone had attacked them in the night, I ran out of the house, and slammed into Caspian.

My face must have shown signs of worry, because his relaxed posture stiffened and his brow narrowed. "What's happened?" he said.

"When did you return?"

"Just now." He smiled. "And I have good news for Agna. Where is she?"

"The house is empty."

"Danica too?"

I nodded, thinking of every possible reason why they could both be gone.

"Do you know where they could have gone? Anyone that they would go to?"

"Agna was worried about her sister. She could have taken her to the willow or maybe her grandmother's?" Worry gripped my heart. The forest may have been cleared of the undead, but that didn't mean we were safe.

"Then we will check both." He clamped a hand on my shoulder.

"Yaya's is on the way. We'll go there first."

I whistled and Fey trotted to my side. Running couldn't take me there fast enough. I left Caspian gasping for air. Sweat slid down my neck, the furs too hot for the weather. Agna would be fine, but part of me worried the past day's events had changed her feelings. While her parent's death had happened many years ago, the return of her father opened an old wound. It brought back the dark memories of that night. The night where Vikings raided and killed.

I was a Viking, from head to feet. Could she ever truly be with me?

Yaya's cottage came into view. "Agna!" I yelled, not slowing for a moment.

The door opened before I could reach her. Her scarf covering her hair blew with the wind. Agna stared at me, wide eyed.

"See, nothing to fear, my friend," Caspian said as he pounded to my side.

He was wrong. I knew Agna. Every expression, every emotion. Fear haunted her face.

"What are you doing here?" she asked, glancing back at the house as she rushed to me.

Caspian walked off to the side to give us privacy.

"You said to come in the morning. You weren't there, either of you."

She tipped her head low and sighed. "I'm sorry. Danica was getting worse and I had to bring her to Yaya."

I grabbed Agna's hand. "Why not bring Yaya to you? Or come get me? It's not safe to travel at night."

She smiled, but would not meet my gaze. "You know how Yaya is. She never wants to stay in the settlement."

She was hiding something. I could tell in how she avoided my eyes as if I would pull the truth from hers. I tugged her forward until her chest touched mine and slid my free hand across the back of her neck. "I can't stop thinking of last night. I was worried I had frightened you."

"You could never frighten me," she whispered back while lifting her gaze to finally meet mine.

Dawn sprinkled into her eyes, lighting the few specks of amber hidden within the deep green. I brought her face close to mine and kissed her. Her mouth only slightly opened, refusing me a deeper kiss. I pulled back, raising a brow at her. "Is everything all right?"

She glanced to Caspian who quickly pretended to examine a leaf.

"Don't mind him. Priests aren't interested in this sort of thing."

Her cheeks flushed and she bit her lip. "And what exactly is that?"

I grinned and brought her back to my lips, ignoring the stare at my back from our Christian friend.

Crash!

Caspian and I looked at each other and I pushed Agna aside.

"It's nothing," she said, holding my arm. "Just Yaya making a mess."

But then a loud scream bellowed from the home.

Agna darted to the house, reaching the door before me and throwing it open. Yaya lay on her back, her rocking chair splintered and lying next to her.

"Yaya!" Agna slid to her side, taking her arm and helping her sit.

The curtain at the one window in the home swayed. I nodded to Caspian to go inspect it, while I ran outside.

The grass by the window had been crushed and a set of footprints led off toward the woods. I slid out my axes and followed the trail.

"Folkvarr! Wait!"

Agna shouted behind me. I stopped and turned around. "Who was in there?" Fury filled my chest. "Was it him? Is that why you snuck over here?"

Her mouth dropped open. "Who are you talking about?"

"I've seen the way he looks at you. His gaze hovers over your every curve." My chest heaved up and down as the words tumbled out in a wave of rage. "You would lie with a spirit, before a man?"

She narrowed her gaze. "Don't you mean *boy*?"

The fire in her eyes matched the flame burning inside me. "Who was here?"

"It's none of your concern." Her words were sharp, and while she held her chin high, she could not hide the tremble of her hands.

I stomped to her, and she jumped as I grabbed her arm. I would never harm her, but I needed the truth. At my touch, her hard expression shattered.

"Tell me," I said.

She shook her head, fighting whatever lie she tried to hide. I let her go. "Fine. I'll track whoever it is myself."

"No!" she cried, pulling my arm. "Just forget it. Everything's fine. Come inside, please." She slid her hand up my arm, tugging at my shirt, and taking me into her embrace. "It was a long night, and right now, all I want is to rest. Will you stay with me?"

With her lips so close to mine, I found it hard to deny her. "If that's what you want."

"I do. I do." She tugged my neck down, bringing me into a deep kiss.

I silently groaned as she held onto me, kissing me deep and fast. Her tongue danced with mine. I tossed my axes to the ground. Whatever person or spirit had been inside Yaya's home, no longer mattered. Agna would tell me why she left without letting me know. I would've helped her bring Danica here.

"Where is your sister?" I broke Agna's spell on me, gauging her response. Her sister wasn't in the house.

"She's . . . feeling better. She wanted some fresh water."

The feigned glance, the tight lines on her head, all signs she lied.

"That's great news," I said, giving a warm smile. "It means you have an empty home." I swept Agna off the grass and into my arms. She squeaked, and smiled.

"We can go now, before Yaya looks for me." She played with my bottom lip, her fingers teasing me.

"Let's tell them where we're going first. I can't leave Caspian with Yaya."

Agna waved a hand. "He'll be fine. Take me now."

Those words taunted my senses, and when she slid her fingers over my mouth, I had to fight every urge raging through me. The soft, hinting way she spoke, enticing me, thinking I couldn't possibly say no.

How she underestimated me.

With a quick grin, I said nothing, and walked back around to the front yard, letting her dance her fingers across my neck. When she realized I was walking back into Yaya's, she gripped my shirt.

"It's silly to waste time. Caspian will be fine." Her voice croaked, just a bit.

"Of course," I said, placing her back on her feet and kissing her nose. "But I want to tell him the same. I promise to make it up to you." I trailed my finger down the front of her dress, stopping just between her ribs. I could feel her fast heartbeat, see the worry in her wide eyes.

Yaya sat in another chair at the small round table, drinking from a wooden cup.

"We have a problem," Caspian whispered as he met me at the door.

I glanced behind me to see Agna rubbing her hands together and looking utterly terrified. "Speak."

"Danica is the witch."

Wait!" Folkvarr charged out the door like a bull. My heart leapt in a wild panic as I chased after him. "Please, wait!"

"You knew?" He spun around, his face contorted in pain. "This whole time you knew. You tricked me."

"No," I pleaded. "I only just learned."

"Another lie." His stormy eyes went cold, sending a shiver down my spine.

"If you'll just listen." I reached for him and he jerked back. "Please, I love you. I didn't know."

The coldness in his eyes broke my heart. Pain cut it into a thousand pieces and the sobs pouring out of me dropped me to my knees. With a quick spin, his back was to me again. He stomped away from Yaya's, tearing apart my heart as he walked. "Folkvarr, please!"

He didn't stop, nor glance back.

I clutched the dirt with my hands, crying into the earth,

begging Perun to fix this. Danica disappeared, though I still didn't know how or why, and now Folkvarr … The last of his fur-lined cape disappeared within the brush. I fell against my hands crying. We were going to marry. Now, now he couldn't bear to look at me.

Ripping pain rumbled through my body until the sobs stopped and numbness filled my limbs. Wiping my tears away, I picked myself up, brushed the dirt off my rubaKHa, and walked into Yaya's.

Yaya sat while Caspian knelt by the broken rocker, trying to fix it.

"What happened?" I needed to understand how my very sick sister, climbed out of a window and ran off into the woods. Before I could fix any of this mess, I had to find her.

"It all happened so fast." Yaya held out her hand to me. "One moment, Danica was sleeping then the next, her eyes were open. She darted out of the bed, scaring me so I fell into the chair. She took off through the window."

"But why?" I stared at the open window. *Where have you gone little sister?*

"Was she sleeping?"

Yaya and I both looked at Caspian. "Yes," I said.

"What happened before Folkvarr and I arrived?"

I thought back, recalling the conversation. "We were talking about Folkvarr. I was worried what would happen if they found out about Danica."

"About her being the witch?"

"Yes, but she was asleep."

"Or pretending." Yaya stood, a hard look on her face.

I refused to believe my sister would pretend to sleep or be sick. "It doesn't matter why she ran. I need to find her. Yaya, was she . . .?"

Yaya smiled. "No, child, she was not turned."

I sighed. "Thank, Perun."

"That's what I came back to tell you." Caspian placed the rocker back and stood. "From what I read, the voldak would have had to drain almost all of her blood to turn, but from your story, you killed it quickly."

"I did." A shiver ran through me as I remembered Papa's fangs on her neck. "I'm going after her."

"I'll go with you," Caspian said.

"No. I'll be fine. If she sees you, she may not speak to me."

"Your sister cast a powerful spell that brought the dead to life. She didn't do it alone, and her reasons must be found out."

"I know." I sighed, understanding the danger Danica had put us all in. "But I need to do this, alone."

"Take Lew—"

"Yes, Yaya." I rolled my eyes and shook my head. "I'll take the blighted ram with me. I'll be back soon."

I raced out the door and over to Lew's gate. I didn't really want to go alone, but if I had any chance of keeping Danica safe. I had to go. I had to find her and discover the truth.

And I had to do it before Folkvarr did.

29

age filled my steps as I stomped over brush and fern, heading back to the settlement. *How could she have lied to me?* While she claimed to have only just learned the truth, I didn't believe her. She knew since the day we ran the inspection. All this time her feelings had been a show. A distraction.

Her lips bore a lie I had believed with my whole heart.

Argh! I swung my axe at a branch, slicing it off. The urge to beat or kill any beast that dared cross my path consumed my thoughts. I would not dwell on her face, nor her eyes that had entranced me into a fool.

No more.

"She's telling the truth."

Kole appeared in front of me, blocking my path. I swung my axes in my hands, giving him a fair warning to step aside.

"Get out of my way, spirit."

He folded his arms. "You really don't believe her?"

"This doesn't concern you." I stepped around him, only so

I wouldn't throw an axe in his chest.

"There is more here than your wounded pride. I saw them last night. Agna was distraught over the truth, and terrified." His eyes flamed brighter, but his cocky grin failed to appear. "And do you know where Agna goes now? She's off to find her sister. She has no idea the danger she walks in to."

"What are you talking about?"

Kole laughed. "You humans don't understand magic or the power it needs. Danica aligned herself with the Jezibaba—the coven of Baba Yaga. They would have had to summon a demon in order to control a horde that big. Do you think the demon has left? And do you think the coven will spare anyone who comes after them? They will unleash the demon and Agna will be slaughtered."

Anger shifted to worry. If Kole spoke truth, Agna could not face that horror. "Why didn't you mention this demon before?"

"There was no proof a witch caused the wake of the dead, but now that I know black magic was used, there's only one coven in this region powerful enough to perform such darkness."

"I must get back to her."

"Better hurry," Kole said. "She's already gone, but don't worry, little Viking, I'll fly ahead and keep my eyes on her."

Kole morphed into a bird, cawing off into the sky. I slung my axes into their holders, and prayed Odin would get me to Agna quickly.

30

Lew shuffled beside me as I attempted to track my sister. Except I had no idea how to track. I had watched Folkvarr do it. He would examine the brush, look for signs of passage, but what signs? How could I know if it wasn't a squirrel or a deer walking this way?

"This is hopeless." I knelt in the brush, picking at a broken twig. "I'll never find her this way. Why couldn't you be a hound."

The old ram blinked an eye and chomped on a nearby fern.

"Need some help, *krasavitza moya*?"

"I'm terrible at tracking." I couldn't hide the relief flooding my soul at the sight of Kole. "Can you track her?"

"Of course." His grin elongated as fangs replaced his white teeth. Black fur sprouted from his skin until the boy became a giant wolf.

He nudged my leg with his nose, turning his head to the side. "What?"

With a low growl, he bent his front legs down, bowed his head, just like when he was an elk. I grabbed the scruff of his neck and lifted myself onto his back. Even though he wasn't as large as the elk, my feet still didn't come close to touching the ground.

With a leap, Kole was off, racing through the brush, I glanced back looking for Lew, but the ram was becoming a small dot in the forest. He would get bored and wander back to Yaya's. I had no fear of the forest creatures messing with that ornery animal.

Gripping the fur with both hands, I leaned forward, pressing my chest against Kole's back. Solid muscle, strength, and the faint scent of pine drifted from his coat. Out of all the leshie in the forest, he had answered my call. He fulfilled his end of the bargain, yet he continued to help us. Why? Was he worried I would run?

I wanted to believe that as a guardian of our land, he cared about its people. Yaya called us children of the forest, the mist our mother, and the willow our ancient protector. If Danica needed to run, or hide, he would help. I just needed to find her first.

Deeper into the forest we went, past the old willow, and past the cave to the rusalki palace. It wasn't until we neared the bank of the river that Kole stopped. The sun lit the quiet place, sparkling the lazy river and heating the rocks by its side.

Though Holmgeirr had been taken farther up the river, the sight of the large boulders and rushing water, reminded me all the same.

I slid off Kole's back and lifted a hand to shield my eyes from the sun-glinted water. "Is there anything over here?"

"The scent ends here." Kole stretched out his body, back in human form. "Danica must have traveled in the water. I can't track her any further. There's no more to do," he added. "So I suggest a swim."

"A swim?" I balked at the idea. "This is not the time to be swimming."

"Of course it is." He slid off his tunic, revealing a chest rippled with muscles. "The trail has gone cold. Swim with me, *krasavitza moya*," he whispered, his mouth curving into a devilish grin.

"I need to look for my sister." I met his intense gaze, ignoring how much closer he moved.

"You won't find her here."

"Then I'll look somewhere else."

"Tsk. Tsk." Kole titled his head, licking his lips like I was lunch.

Since that first day we met, the two of us had never been alone again. His striking eyes sent a wave of uncertainty through me.

Don't trust him.

"Are you going to help me or not?" My voice cracked as his eyes flashed red.

"Yes, but as I said before, trail ends here, *lyubimaya*."

Beloved? "You really shouldn't say those things."

He leaned over, angling his body to gaze straight into my eyes. Our noses almost touched. "I will say whatever I like. You belong to me, not him." With a wink, he ran into the water and dove in.

Heat rushed through my face, my body. I wanted to cry, scream, punch the ground so hard the sky cried. Everything was a game to him, constantly calling me, my beauty, and now beloved?

This has gone on too long. I must tell Yaya what I bargained.

Or . . .

A terrible, terrible thought entered my mind. I didn't want to even suggest it, but what if the witches were powerful enough to break the oath? If I could find Danica before Folkvarr, maybe she could help. With the oath broken, Folkvarr and I could be together.

Though the witches would surely want something in return then I'd be back in the same trouble.

I slid off my shoes and sat by the river. The heat beat against my face. With the trail gone, I should've returned to the settlement, but I wasn't ready to face Folkvarr yet.

I still couldn't understand how Danica could be involved with dark magic. When Papa returned from the dead, clawing, and ready to drag us into his nightmare, the fear and shock on her face, the longing She'd had no idea he would return. If she had, she would have been prepared.

Why, Danica? What have you gotten yourself into?

Kole poked his head out of the water. "You really must come in." He swiped a hand through his hair. The sun's rays danced on his eyes, igniting the fire within them. Handsome, very, but I would never get closer than I needed to.

"I'm fine here," I replied, though the heat beat on my face and sweat began to pool at the base of my neck. I wanted to swim. I *needed a* swim.

I took off the temple rings holding my kerchief in place. At least with the fabric off my head, my scalp could breathe.

"Only a few more items to remove." Kole back stroked in

the water, grinning at me.

The desire to wade into the cool water, overcame the worry of what tricks Kole might pull once I entered. "If I come in, you are not allowed to come near me. Understood?"

"Of course," he said, continuing to smile. "I'll stay right here."

I undid the apron, but left my rubaKHa on. Kole saw me once in my undergarments, and that was enough.

"You're not swimming in that, are you?" He pointed at the dress.

"Of course," I chirped back.

He laughed. "Have fun, but you'll sink."

Sink? What did he know?

I stepped into the river. The cold tickled my skin. I stepped in farther, enjoying the break from the heat. Once the water reached my waist, I dove forward and fanned out my arms. The heat dissipated as cool, refreshing water soothed my skin. I lay on my back, dipping my arms into the river and pushing myself around. No clouds filled the sky. A perfect day.

Almost perfect.

Birds sang from the nearby trees, relaxing my body so much that I closed my eyes and tried to think of a time before the undead, when Danica and I would play in the river after washing our clothes. How she would laugh and dunk me under until I splashed her so hard, she couldn't stop laughing. That was the sister I needed. Our parent's death pained her much, but it did the same to me, yet she had turned to darkness.

How did Danica get involved with a coven? It had to be someone who hated Vikings so fiercely they would go to any length to remove them from our lands, including dealing with a coven of witches.

But many Slavic people felt that way. Too many.

The river moved faster, and I noticed I had waded quite a bit from Kole. *Better not get too far.* I swam closer to the bank where a large tree had fallen. Using its trunk for support, I pulled myself along its side, edging to the riverbank.

A deep rumble sounded from up the river. I squinted at the distance, but saw nothing.

"Agna?" Kole waded out of the river, calling for me.

"Here!" I shouted back.

The rumble sounded again, louder this time.

"Get out!" he yelled and began running down the bank toward me.

I swiftly waded through the water, but was yanked back. Leaning down, I reached for whatever branch had caught me, but my fingers couldn't find anything.

The lazy river began rushing past me, suddenly powerful and fast.

"Agna, move!"

"I can't!" I tugged at my rubaKHa trying to break it free. "I'm stuck!"

Kole reached the bank's edge and dove in. Within moments, he reached me.

"My rubaKHa." I pulled at the fabric again, but it did not give.

He nodded and dove under the water. He pulled at my stuck clothes while I watched the river; a massive rush of brown water tumbled forward.

Mudslide.

I hit the top of Kole's back, urging him to be quicker. "Hurry!"

Closer the tumult of water came, violent, muddy, and fast. Broken trees and grass whirled inside the water, rolling closer. Within minutes, it would sweep us both away.

"Kole!" I screamed, eyes wide as the wave hit us like stone then I lost myself in the rushing river, drowning in it.

31

Caspian left Yaya's and followed me after Agna. Her clumsy steps had left an easy trail to follow, until her tracks disappeared beside a set of giant paw marks.

Kole.

Fury rose in my chest, thinking of Agna running with that wild spirit. Kole showed to be an ally, but why? If he had fulfilled his end of the bargain, he had no reason to stay around Agna, unless he wanted something else.

"The tracks go past there," I said to Caspian. We ran after the broken brush left in Kole's passing until we reached the riverbank.

The river rushed by us fast, too fast for them to have crossed. I looked up then down. Where could they be? "Do you see that?" In the distance, I saw a shadow on the ground.

Caspian nodded. "It looks like someone."

Using my hand to shield the sun, I squinted. "Two of them. And one's not moving." I raced down the river's bank, never taking my eyes off the scene unfolding before me.

Agna lay on her back, Kole kissing her.

"What are you doing to her?" I yelled at Kole, ready to rip him apart, but Caspian grabbed my arms.

"Wait," Caspian said. "She's not breathing."

"What did you say?" I spun around at Caspian whose gaze fixated on Kole.

Caspian ignored me and knelt on the opposite side of Agna. He grabbed his cross, immediately chanting. I watched in horror, everything slowing before me. A pale blue light emanated around Kole's mouth as he continued to keep his mouth over hers. He pulled back, spitting water onto the ground, then went back to breathing that strange light into her.

She can't be gone. Emptiness flooded my soul as I watched the girl I loved, fade away. My limbs froze in place. A fog clouded over me, every part of my being going numb. Caspian's voice rose in crescendo. He swung his wooden cross above her lifeless body, back and forth.

She's dead. And it's my fault.

If I had listened. If I had stopped to listen to her pleas.

For all my strength, I was helpless.

"Come on!" Kole screamed after spitting more water onto the ground.

I did this.

This is my fault.

Agna coughed, and Kole turned her on her side where she spit up water. He slapped her back. She gagged and spewed more fluid then took several ragged breaths. She leaned into him, heaving, her body shaking

"Close one," he said, wrapping an arm around her waist.

Relief flooded through me. "Agna!"

She turned to me, coughing, her eyes glistening. Her dress had been shredded, revealing her shivering legs. I knelt by her side and gently pulled her away from Kole. In my arms, she burst into tears, hugging me and digging her face into my chest. I stroked her head, whispering over and over again that she was safe.

"What happened?" Caspian asked as I didn't have the words to speak.

"We were trying to cross the river and her rubaKHa got caught." Kole leaned back on his heels and wiped his brow. "The storm last night must've caused a mudslide, though I find it odd just to appear now. I barely got her free in time."

"Do you think it was Danica?" Caspian stood, dusting the dirt off his robe.

Kole followed. "No. Danica may be in league with the coven, but she's not powerful enough to create a storm. I'm going up the river to investigate."

"I'll go with you," Caspian added, earning an arched brow from Kole. "If we run into Danica, maybe I can talk to her, before things get worse. Also, it's not safe for any of us to be alone."

Kole grinned. "Thank you. I appreciate the help."

Caspian missed the flash in Kole's eyes. *That priest has no idea what he's in for.* While Kole may have ill will toward me, I sensed the priest amused him.

Agna shivered in my arms. "I'm freezing."

Caspian took off his cloak and wrapped it around her. "We'll come back as soon as we find something."

Kole nodded, and there was no grin or snide remark. Worry creased his brow as he stared at Agna. "Go."

I cradled Agna in my arms. "I'll see you soon."

With Agna in my arms, I began the long walk back. She shivered, but slowly, relaxed. I wanted to apologize for storming away earlier. I should have listened to her story, believed her, but the shock that her own blood had betrayed her . . . it was too much for me to bear. If it had been one of my brothers, I wouldn't have worried about his well-being. His last memory would be my axes in his chest. There could be no room for mercy or sympathy when blood betrays their own.

I thought of my younger brothers, still at home with mother and our sister. Not old enough to fight. If either one had done such a dark thing, would I really be able to make that blow? End their life forever? I'd like to think I could stay true to our way, but I understood the burden of being the oldest. We had a responsibility for our younger siblings. Did Agna blame herself for this? I hoped not.

We passed Yaya's. I thought of stopping, but the strain of carrying Agna burned my muscles. I continued on, focusing on the short distance left, instead of the ache spreading through my arms. Soft breaths left Agna's lips. Sometime during the journey, she had fallen asleep.

Using my side, I pushed open her door. Her bed sat against the far left wall. I eased her on it and grabbed the blanket to cover her with. "You're safe now." I dragged the chair from the table and sat next to her.

"I'm sorry." Her lips trembled. "I should have told you as soon as I learned the truth."

"Shhh." I placed a finger against her lips. "Sleep. We can talk later."

She sighed and slowly blinked her eyes. "Okay."

I pushed her wet hair off her forehead and back behind her ears. Coldness painted her skin. I looked for another blanket and dropped it on top of her, but with her dress soaking wet she would never get warm.

"Agna," I said softly, bending over to her. "Can you get out of your dress? You're still freezing."

"I think so." She yawned and shivered, raising up on an elbow. "I'll start a fire."

I went over to her fire pit, searching for the tinder and striker. Once I found both, I ignited the twigs and the fire crackled alive. When I turned around, Agna lay back on the bed, still dressed.

Gently, I helped her sit, and cupped her face. "You have to undress."

She leaned against my shoulder. "I'm so tired."

Worry panicked in my heart. The water was cold, but not so cold she would die, still, I knew enough that she needed to get warm.

I'll have to do it myself, then.

"Try and not fall asleep again." She yawned, curling against me. I pushed her upright and tugged at the fabric at her waist, pulling it up. With barely open eyes, she raised her arms and I lifted the dress off.

Droplets of water slipped against her skin. The slip she wore stuck to her, showing off all the curves I had fantasized about. Staring at the rise and fall of her chest, I lost myself. A deep hunger rolled through me, warming my body at the sight of her perfect breasts. I traced a hand up her bare shoulder and neck. My breath caught in my throat as goose bumps rose against her skin.

Lifting her face to mine, I crushed my lips against hers. She kissed me back softly, lazily. When I pulled back, her eyes closed. I kissed her cheek then gently laid her back on the bed. No matter how intense the desire to be with her was, she needed to rest, and if I cared for her at all, I needed to give it to her.

With a heavy breath, I reached for the blankets, wrapped them around her shivering body, and moved her closer to the fire. If I couldn't be with her, I'd hold her, until the warmth returned.

Curled in my lap, falling fast asleep, Agna's shivers stopped. The fire popped and cracked, warming the home, and sending me into a deep rest with her.

32

olkvarr's warm breath tickled my neck. He lay curled behind me, tiny snores escaping his lips. I pulled his arms around me tighter, enjoying the warmth from his body.

I guess this means things are okay.

I kissed the soft spot on the inside of his bicep. We had come too close to losing it all. My mind raced with worry. Yes, Folkvarr was here, but that didn't mean he wasn't still angry with me. I wanted to wake him and tell him over and over again, I hadn't known Danica was the witch.

"You're awake." He nuzzled my neck with his nose. "How are you feeling?"

"Better." I leaned back into him and he squeezed me tighter.

"I thought I lost you." His voice dropped into a whisper.

Turning around, I faced him. "I'm sorry. I didn't know. I swear."

"Shhh." Touching a finger to my lips, he kept me from speaking. "I believe you."

"What do we do now?"

His lips curled into a grin. "I can think of a few things."

It was then I realized I was still in my slip. One thin piece of fabric keeping us apart. As if Folkvarr sensed my thoughts, he trailed his fingers across my cheek, down my neck, dancing across my skin.

A flame ignited inside me, and I brought his face to mine. He kissed me, then pulled away to nibble the bottom of my lip and my chin. Returning to my lips, he kissed me deeply again. His slow, deliberate moves teased me until the tiny flame turned into an inferno of want and need.

In a swift daring move, I pushed him back on the bed, and rolled on top of him. His eyes widened and he gripped my waist. I bit my lip, but only to stop myself from laughing.

"How far does the raven go?" This time, I trailed my fingers across him, drawing a line down his neck and under his shirt. His chest rose and fell, and he gazed at me, silent, waiting.

"Does it go all the way down?" I dragged my pointer down the front of his shirt right to his belly button.

He growled and sat up, almost toppling me backward in the process, but he wrapped one arm around me, catching me. "Playing games?"

With my legs wrapped around him, I knew this was a *very* dangerous game.

"Maybe," I chirped, brushing off the moment and ignoring how my heart pounded.

He ran his hand up my waist, up my chest, until he clenched my neck. "I don't like to lose."

Mother of the woods was I in trouble.

He pulled me to his lips, and I let him take back control, losing myself in the idea that soon we would be husband and wife. No matter what my aunt or anyone else said, Folkvarr and I were going to be together for eternity, and no one would stop that. Not Kole. Not even Perun himself.

Folkvarr played with every part of me, my mind, my soul, my body. Closing my eyes, I let go of the worry and fear and panic that had consumed me for too long. I let the softness of his lips take me away into the netherworld. I let his kisses wash away the hurt and ache of loss. I let his hands hold me, and reassure me I was safe.

A knock sounded on the door, interrupting our magical moment.

"Agna, Danica, are you home?"

My body froze at the sound of Aunt Jasna's voice. Folkvarr met my shocked expression with his own. I knew she would come, but now? So soon?

"Agna? Are you in there?" She banged again and I was thankful Folkvarr had barred the door and the window shutter was closed. "They must be out. We can check back later."

"And you're sure she's aware of our arrival? I have business in Kiev and cannot be detained much longer."

Folkvarr's fingers dug into me at the sound of an unfamiliar male voice.

"Of course," Aunt Jasna said. "She still has her morning duties to attend. Come, let me show you the rest of the village. There's an old woman who bakes the most delightful meat pie."

The voices drifted away, and I released the breath I had been holding. Folkvarr slid out from under me and picked up his belt and strapped on his axes.

"What are we going to do?" I ran to grab a rubaKHa from under the bed and slipped it on. "We can't hide from her."

Folkvarr's brow furrowed as he tightened his belt and buttoned his tunic.

"Folkvarr!"

"I'm thinking!"

Now dressed, I lifted the plank off the holder and slowly creaked open the door.

"Hello."

I gasped at Caspian's sudden appearance, and dragged him inside the house.

"What are you doing?" I hissed at him, holding the door shut with my body.

"I've come to tell you Kole has a lead." His gazed wandered to me and Folkvarr. "Is something wrong?"

Folkvarr's jaw twitched.

"Yes," I said. "My Aunt has paid a dowry for me, and the suitor is here to collect. I won't marry him."

"Would you marry someone else?" Caspian's eyes twinkled, and I didn't miss the hint of a smile.

I reached back to grab Folkvarr's hand. "Yes. There's most certainly someone else."

"Then I will marry you. Kole said he wouldn't be back until dusk. We have plenty of time." Caspian clapped his hands. "Shall we begin?"

"Wait!" I glanced back at Folkvarr, hoping he wouldn't take my hesitation as a sign that I didn't want to. "I . . ." How could I explain that having a quick ceremony in the home where my parents were killed and where my undead father tried to kill me was not where I wanted to be wed.

"The willow." Folkvarr squeezed my hand.

I nodded, and jumped at him. He wrapped his arms around me.

"Are we really going to do this, now?" I searched his stormy eyes and all I found was love.

"If you're ready, I am." He said it with so much conviction, I knew we could conquer anything.

"We'll need a witness," Caspian said.

"Yaya. I'll go to Yaya and you can meet me at the willow."

Folkvarr grimaced. "I don't know if that's a good idea. We should stick together."

I kissed his lips. "I want to talk to her alone. I'll be safe."

He kissed me back. "Then I will see you soon."

With another quick kiss, I was out the door and racing toward Yaya's. My heart exploded with happiness, so much, I couldn't help but laugh and squeal all the way through the forest. Yaya would give us her blessing. I knew she would.

Danica and I couldn't be unwed forever, and there was no one else I would give my heart and body to. It was Folkvarr or no one.

When Yaya's home came into view, I ran faster, desperate to share my good news.

Her door swayed open. The wind blew it back and forth, knocking it against the house.

"Yaya!" I pounced up the two steps and into her home.

Blood splattered the floor. Splattered the walls. The air stank of death, leaving a metallic taste in my mouth. The table and chairs were smashed and splintered all throughout the home. Every kerchief and every beautiful blanket she had sewn, dotted with death. A massacre.

"Yaya?" I glanced around, but the only remnant of her was the knitting she worked on, tossed on the floor and drenched in red. "Yaya!"

I dashed back outside and around to Lew's gate. There, lying face down in the dirt, was my beloved Yaya.

"No!" I fell beside her and turned over her body.

Her green eyes were wide and empty. Her skin cold to touch. Blood trickled out of her nose and mouth. I gathered her into my arms, sobbing, every part of me ripping with anger. How? *How?*

"I'm so sorry." Danica's voice cut through my misery.

I glanced to the left, to see her crying and holding her hands to her mouth. "I didn't know they would kill her."

Anger, deep and roaring rose within me. "You did this? You killed our Yaya?"

She shook her head. "Never! It was them. They did it!" Danica's eyes were red and her face blotched. "I would never have agreed to help, if I knew Yaya would be at risk!" Her voice screeched, and she sobbed harder, rising to her feet.

I kissed the top of Yaya's head, closed her eyes, and gently laid her back down on the grass. "You will fix this." I rose to meet Danica, balling my fists. "Bring her back!"

"I can't." Danica stepped closer.

My fists shook at my sides. I wanted to hit her, to hurt her, but she was my sister. And Yaya . . .

"Agna, please. I would never endanger any of you. *Please!*"

Her begging did no good. Yaya was gone!

Danica's eyes went wide. "You mustn't harm her!" Danica's gaze went behind me. "She's protected by the coven!"

I turned around just in time to see a massive, black monster descend on me.

33

I always knew I would marry, though I never imagined what it would be like. How I could be filled with anxious thoughts, how my palms would sweat, and how every moment that passed, all I could think of was how Agna would be all mine.

No other girl had embedded herself into my mind the way Agna had. So much it was distracting. Most of my waking thoughts were of Agna. I wanted to kiss every part of her skin. To hear only my name on her lips. I would spend the rest of our days, pleasing her, and building a family that would be a symbol of peace between our people.

Caspian leaned against the tree, humming or chanting, or mumbling. "Are you nervous?" he asked.

"No."

He grinned and I ignored his raised brow.

"Wouldn't any man be nervous on their wedding day?"

"So you are going to marry the Slav."

Flo walked out of the woods and into the clearing. He

squinted at the Will-O-Wisps that rapidly flew up into the leaves.

"Did you follow me?" I eyed Flo carefully.

He slid his hands into the folds of his cape. "You and Caspian left so quickly, I only assumed you had a lead on the witch." He walked closer. "But if that were true, why would you not come for good old Flo?"

I stood taller, holding my chin up and meeting his stare. "What I do in my own time, is my business."

"Tsk. Tsk." Flo's lip curled, and he tilted his head at me, watching me like prey. "And what happens when the marriage is set? Will she travel to Novgorod with us? The road is long and we don't travel with wenches."

Heat boiled my blood, heating me through. "Watch your tongue."

"She is very pretty and kind, but she is not meant for the road."

"But she's meant to fight undead and travel with us when it's useful?"

Flo shrugged. "Maybe, though I think your bride to be is having second thoughts. Shouldn't she be here, already?"

The sun had moved closer to dusk. She should have been back with Yaya already.

"I'm going to Yaya's to see what's holding her up." I pushed past Flo, ignoring the sneer on his face. He could think what he wanted, but I was marrying Agna.

The three of us sprinted through the woods, Caspian rambling about what he discovered about the voldak. I couldn't care less about his brethren's theories. The sun's rays were dying and Agna hadn't come. Sure, she could have changed her mind, but I feared the worst.

I feared her aunt had found her, and somehow taken her away from me.

We shouldn't have separated.

Flo entertained Caspian's ramblings, all the while sneering when glancing my way. I don't think he truly cared who I married, but he knew my father, and if my father had already set a precedent, Flo blindly obeyed.

A loud bleat sounded from my left as Lew crashed through the woods. We were still a bit from Yaya's. What was Lew doing out this far?

"Everything good, boy?" I bent over and met his big black eyes. He bleated again and the sound sent a shiver down my spine. In all the chaos the ram had been through, I'd never found him so desperate.

I sprinted toward Yaya's. The mist thickened as we encroached on Yaya's home, covering the ground in a thick blanket. The empty quiet of the woods and Yaya's swinging door, made every hair on my body stand on end.

"Something is wrong here." Caspian held out his cross.

Blood trickled across the ground, leading straight to a body.

Yaya.

Caspian ran to her side as I watched, frozen in place. He checked her mouth for breath, but I could already tell by Yaya's paled skin she was gone.

"What happened to her?" Flo leaned over Yaya, inspecting the wounds across her chest and neck. "Was this a voldak?"

"Where is Agna?" I said as Caspian, Flo, and I all exchanged looks.

A black wolf burst out of the trees, nearly toppling over Caspian in the process. The large beast landed in the center of us, growling, fangs dripping with saliva. Its eyes flashed red.

Kole.

"Where is she?" I asked, gripping my axes.

Kole howled and leapt into the woods.

"Follow him," I said, trying to hide the panic in my voice. It was not our custom to show fear, but with Agna missing and Yaya slaughtered, I found it hard to keep my emotion reigned in.

Waves of nausea crashed into me as we sped throughout the thick brush. Caspian pleaded for us to slow down as we made our way deeper into the dense forest. Flo ran neck and neck with me, jumping and dodging many obstacles, this dark place held for us.

Ahead, the trees opened to a marsh like bog, a pungent odor assaulted our nostrils as we drew closer. Fey growled low at my left flank—he must have caught the scent of something.

"I am not built like you two," Caspian sputtered as he finally caught up to us. "Please, keep that in mind!"

"Too many days spent in your fancy monastery," Flo said teasing the winded priest.

Fey howled into the night air, and in the distance a return howl echoed throughout the crag encrusted swampland. Mounds of rock and dirt frequently dotted the muddy waters of the bog, and Fey bounced from one pile of rock and dirt to another.

Waist deep in muck, I fought against the thick mud, using my strength to push through the brackish liquid. My thoughts stayed focused on Agna, my despair turning into a burning rage. These fiendish beasts had taken so much from me and my people. She had to be alive.

I would not accept any other reality.

Flo half dragged Caspian by the collar, towing the priest through the dark waters of the swamp. Stumbling and sinking into the filthy sludge more than once, the priest weathered the trek in silence. His grim-face remained tight lipped as he fought through the suction like mud.

Behind us the forest disappeared, replaced by spindly thin trees and mist. The mist curled its fingers over everything, shadowing the world around us until we could barely see a few feet ahead. Wading farther into the rock-lined marsh, the mud finally gave way to granite.

Again, Fey howled, and this time the reply sounded close. We all looked up to see a jet-black wolf crying out to the silvery moon. Its supernatural frame stood next to a large dead willow tree, above an insidious cave entrance. Moss and thorn riddled roots covered the mouth of the massive burrow.

"A road to the underworld," Kole said after shapeshifting back into his humanoid form.

"Beelzebub!" Caspian shouted in Kole's direction. I thought Caspian would faint from the shrill he released.

"Do not confuse me with such a filthy mongrel, mortal," Kole hissed.

"Both of you calm down. This is neither the time nor place," I said sternly drawing a smirk from Kole.

"You knew this whole time?" Caspian whirled around to face me, his eyes wide and mouth hanging open in shock.

"Relax, priest," Flo said with a gruffness in his voice. "The creature has saved your life, more than once I'd gather."

"He's in league with the devil!"

"I'm the devil," Flo said with a deep laugh. A wicked grin covered his face as he turned, heading directly into the maw of the dank cave.

"Stay here if you'd like, but we're going in with or without you." My tone was harsher than intended, but Agna could be in grave peril. I had no time to delay.

I could feel Kole's smile at my back, and the grumbling of the disgruntled priest let me know Caspian had made his choice. We would surely need his magic in the fight ahead.

Light left the depths of the cave, leaving us in a darkness black as obsidian.

Caspian chanted behind us, and at the end he distinctly said, "Take flight little ones and lead the way."

A swarm of fireflies flew forth, illuminating the cavern before us. Dimly lit stalagmites covered the uneven floor. A wafting stench of death and decay, permeated into every inch of the wretched den. Bones and rotting flesh littered the rough walkway that slanted deeper into the earth, spiraling into Hel itself.

Up ahead the sounds of a large commotion drew near. "Stay away from her. This wasn't our deal!"

My blood boiled at Danica's voice, overshadowed by the fact Agna was alive, but in danger. Without hesitation, I sprinted ahead, speeding toward the din ahead of me. The cave narrowed and descended into a winding spiral.

Turning around a bend of the serpentine-like cave, the tunnel opened into a fire-lit room thirty feet below me. The path ran the outskirt of the den's exterior walls, ramping down to the floor below. Rope bridges ran across to other plateaus and tunnel entrances of the enormous room where makeshift ladders connected the different levels, some descending to the floor beneath me, and others to vantage points above us I could barely see.

And filling all the spaces in between—the voldak.

In the center of the main level, a haggard, old crone, draped in a blood-soaked robe, shuffled toward the two sisters. Agna lay behind Danica's feet, unmoving, while the young witch stood protectively in front of her with a makeshift club, swinging it wildly as the crone stalked forward. The crone's blade gleamed from the reflected light of the fire.

Methodically, the hag crept around a large black cauldron that seemed to be responsible for the cave's foul odor. Limbs and heads floated in its greenish boiling ichor. It popped and hissed with a dim glow.

The decrepit witch cackled, black ooze drooling from her grotesque teeth and mangled mouth. Deep, heavy eye sockets housed milky-white eyes where no pupil or retina could be seen. Blood caked her white stringy mane that flowed greasily behind her.

"Stay away from her you foul wretch!" Flo, Kole, and Caspian entered the room just as the words left my mouth.

"Blasphemers! How dare you enter this sacred shrine." The crone wheezed and shifted her blind gaze to us. "Kill them!" she shrieked in a high-pitched voice, her face contorting into a twisted mask of rage as she immediately moved her hands in quick patterns.

"Baba Yaga," Kole said with disgust in his tone.

It was the most emotion I had seen the leshii show since

I have known him. By the way his face twisted and his eyes blazed red, I knew the two were mortal enemies.

I wasn't surprised when he leapt from the perch and touched down on the rim of the caldron closest to the hag. His grace and precision landed him with a focused force that toppled the vat over as he dismounted, twisting into a backflip over the grimacing witch. The boiling contents rushed forth, spilling in a deadly deluge toward the sorceress.

"Remember me, crone?" Kole spat as the hag turned into a gaseous form, the scalding liquid of the caldron passing through her harmlessly.

Without stopping, Kole dodged, springing away from the dangerous splash.

From the myriad of tunnels, the voldak raced forward, armed with various swords, maces, and any other weapon you could imagine. Five were already on the rope bridge closest to us and barreling in.

"Go save the girl!" Flo shouted, storming the bridge. He beheaded the first creature while severing the right hand cable at the same time. The bridge shifted as it came apart. Flo grabbed the remaining hand cable, also gaining a foothold on the rope beneath it.

Falling to the floor below, one of the creature's landed directly on a stalagmite, its jagged tip driving through its spine and out through its gut, in a shower of gore.

Flo fought his way to the other side. He had never looked so happy in all the time I've known him. "Come meet your demise," he shouted as he tore into the undead ranks.

Caspian stayed close on my heels, Fey on his. "Watch the

priest, boy," I said to the wolf.

A low growl let me know he would do so, but wasn't happy about the command. Rushing around the path and to the floor, we were greeted by a score of voldak. It was then I saw him, behind the mob of undead, waiting for me with a lifeless expression on his face.

"Poppa." I hadn't called him that since I was a small lad. Seeing him standing there, knowing what that truth meant, filled me such hopelessness. I froze.

I failed him.

Emptiness filled his gaze and strange black lines covered his skin. He shuffled with the flow of voldak. If my father were alive, all those creatures would be dead, and he would be racing toward me.

They turned him.

Fey darted past me, snapping and clawing into the voldak in front of me, bringing me back to the fight. Cross slashing, my blades hacked through the first assailant and sent it reeling backwards, crashing into the tide of undead. Caspian placed a hand on my back, chanting the familiar prayer to his god.

Fire coursed through my veins, invigorating me with a feeling of indestructible power. Charging forward, I cut through the voldak's ranks, slashing and hacking in a wild frenzy. Spinning down the ramp like a razor wind cyclone, I sent limbs flying in a corpse shower.

A wave of terror slammed into my chest as a creature consisting of dark fire and ash, rose from behind my father, striking out with its spectral might. Dark tentacles, the size of small boars, wreathed in black flames, sped toward me.

I thought I was dead until Fey jumped in front of me and absorbed the blow. Black fire surrounded his lifeless body and spun him in a cartwheel past me.

"Fey!" Before I could run after him, the demon released a second blast of magic.

I ducked and rolled out of the way before it could make contact. Caspian, was not as lucky, but the resolute priest absorbed the attack, holding firmly to his holy symbol even as his left arm tore clean from his body. The obsidian inferno dissipated off the flashing energy shield he had managed to conjure.

The voldak in the path of the demon's attack were reduced to a dust cloud of white hot motes. If I hadn't been quick enough I would be dead. I didn't have the luxury of time to contemplate it or Fey as my Father's axe swung in with frightening speed.

Rolling to my feet, I met a barrage of blows, all fierce in their strike, but also familiar. An attack routine I had practiced against most of my life. Though the strikes came in with murderous intent, I knew where they were going.

"Father!" I pleaded with him, begging him to stop.

His empty gaze locked on me. The black lines on his face pulsed.

I don't understand. Agna said her father knew her. He had spoken to her. Is my father not turned?

Through the sequence we went, my mind racing with the memories of the days we would spend practicing. I always thought he was pushing me too hard, expecting unrealistic outcomes. I realized in this moment, he was preparing me for a day such as this, and this was his way of saying goodbye.

I shook it from my head. *I'm not ready to say goodbye.*

He saw my hesitation, and attacked with a shoulder rush. A move he hadn't used before, nor the head butt after it, which smashed my nose and sent me flying.

Keep your head and wits in the fight, distraction leads to death. Year after year, my father pounded those words into my head, and I just had a reminder why.

Lying on my back, I saw Flo above, bloodied but still plenty of life in his furiously moving frame as he hurled a body between me and my father. Flo was always watching my back.

"Careful boy, that's no longer your father," he shouted from above.

This time I had to rise above the boy. If I didn't, then none of us would leave this place. I was prepared to die, but Agna would perish and I couldn't allow that.

Rolling backwards, I pushed myself into a handstand and sprung back to my feet. I caught a quick glimpse of Kole slashing at the crone with his two short swords while leaping over her. Gusts of fire scorched the rock wall where he had just been. He was far more agile and capable of maneuvering around such a deadly array of spells. I had to trust in his hatred for the witch, and from the fire blazing in his eyes, he was in this fight till the end.

As soon as my feet touched the ground, my father forced me on the defensive with a downpour, raining in a torrent of vicious assaults. These weren't a routine, but murderous rage.

How are we going to survive this?

Blood gushed from Caspian's grievous wound, leaving

puddles around his feet. He chanted a powerful hymn, his voice loud and unstopping. The demon relentlessly assaulted him with a savage ferocity. Blow after blow, sparks of multicolored electric plasma exploded off and around the globe of shimmering energy encasing the priest, showering over the battlefield.

In the heart of chaos, and for the first time in my life, I was alone in the fight. The thought of Fey's lifeless body and my brothers surrounded by death, welled a pool of rage inside. A fine focus cleared my mind. Everything slowed, becoming crystal clear. The entire room came into my awareness, and I knew where every lunge and stab would come from.

Lightning reactions from thunderous thoughts, I moved on instinct. Intuition spun me as I launched my offhand axe at the voldak about to run Flo through from his back side— all while keeping my other hand axe perfectly positioned to deflect my father's continuing attack. Spinning head over handle, the streaking axe blade drove into the side of the undead's head, knocking him off the dais. Flo flashed a grin of appreciation in my direction.

My father's heavy, cleaving strikes swept back and forth, forcing me to retreat. I didn't want to kill him. How could I? But to even survive this fight, I had to bring him to unfavorable terrain. Around the tipped vat, the ground was slick. Kole had drawn the witch away from the open space, using the many stone stanchions and stalagmites that filled the cave as cover. Booming clamor echoed throughout the cavern as the wounded hag let off a volley of arcane devastation. Debris fell from the ceiling as her primordial power shook the granite pillars of rock which supported the cave. Kole had to stop her, or we would all be buried alive in this forsaken tomb.

The tipped cauldron gave me the perfect obstacle for slowing my father's relentless stalk. His rage and merciless assault fueled him forward, and he paid for it, slipping on the slick liquid around the large kettle.

Just as I thought I had the situation in better standing, Flo came from above dragging a pile of voldak with him and crashed hard into the stone floor. The priest would call it a miracle that the warrior not only survived the plummet, but rolling from the impact, arrived at my feet with a wide smile on his face.

"I figured I'd bring the party to you," Flo said, adrenaline twitching behind the insane look in his eyes.

Flo and I stood back to back, hacking and slashing away from the caldron's area. Danica had managed to drag Agna to the back of the cave, but if we stayed where we were, they would be caught in the murderous tide of battle.

Odin give me strength.

Rushing in from our sides and dropping down from above, the horde of undead fiends inundated us. We moved into the tighter part of the room where columns of rock gave our flanks more protection. But it was leading us back to the aberration that relentlessly clawed at Caspian's dome of protection. In the tunnels to our right, Kole's laughter and taunts echoed off the walls, along with explosions of magical might accompanied by the witch's shrills of rage.

Calamity engulfed the den. We were going to die.

My father's hulking figure stood out behind the mob of

voldak coming at us. I had no choice. I would not allow his memory to be tarnished as an undead minion, a puppet of some demonic master. No, I would send my father to Valhalla where he belonged.

And if I died in the process, so be it.

"Flo, in life my brother, it has been an honor to fight at your side," I yelled to the berserk warrior who was unleashing total carnage on any voldak close to his deadly radius. "In death grant me one wish."

A glance was all I needed to know he had heard and acknowledged my request. As if he knew what I was about to say, the raging battle frenzy that was Flo, drew most of the crowd to him, shouting a battle cry that would have made Odin envious.

The voldak perceived him as the biggest threat, and it was understandable as he had already decimated more than a third of their swelling number. Caspian's shield winked in and out of existence. Soon the ash demon would turn to us and none would survive.

Five voldak stood between me and my father.

Bursting into motion, my intent was murder. I would not be stopped.

I couldn't let my father live as one of these creatures.

Side stepping the first attack, a voldak came in with a downward chop. Grabbing the top of its wrist as the blade harmlessly passed me, I took the sword from its hand as my axe took the arm off at the elbow. Lunging into bite at my neck, the undead caught my upswing in his mouth severing the top of its skull clean off. The second abomination was more skilled, but my newly acquired sword swiftly rose, parrying its diagonal slash. Crossing one arm over the other, I buried my axe deep in the creature's face, killing it on impact.

My father's rage equaled my own. He cleaved the last two behind the lone voldak between us in a crazed attempt to get to me, as if his sole purpose was to kill me.

Kicking the beast in the back, the voldak came barreling in at me, a diversion for the killing blow which undoubtedly was following. He was still my father after all, and way deadlier than I could hope to be. Strafing right, I drove my newly gained sword into the creature's chest allowing it to fly past me, as the human projectile sailed through the air. Leaving the blade buried in the creature's torso, I barely moved my shoulder away from my father's crushing blow.

Pain flared in my arm as he cut deep into the back of my left forearm. The gash sank to the bone, but thankfully I had moved fast enough to save the arm from being completely lost. Blood ran freely and my left hand tingled, before losing all feeling. He backhanded me to the side. I hit the floor and rolled sideways as a series of vicious blows rained from above, causing sparks to fly as his blade smashed off rock.

A stalagmite stopped my roll, leaving me in a dire situation: A dead end that would end my life. I held my breath as my father's strike came in—this was going to hurt.

A familiar ball of fur, one who had saved my life so many times, flew through the air, catching the axe shaft in its side, yelping as the blow crushed Fey's ribs, sending him flying once again. The absorption of the strike allowed me to jump to my feet and catch the handle with my one good hand.

Rolling my arm and driving the axe down, I elbowed my father in his face with everything I had left in me. Staggering back, I saw a glimmer of recognition in his eyes as the black lines on his face began receding.

I shot a glance toward Caspian. Glowing white and doubled his normal size, he had the demon by the throat, squeezing the life from it.

I glanced back to my father who was pulling out one of my axes that had been lodged in a voldak's head. Somehow my father was tied to the demon.

This was my chance, but what if Caspian prevailed? What if once the demon was destroyed, my father returned?

And what if he didn't?

Never hesitate in battle, right, Father?

Consciousness began slipping from me. I swayed on my feet, having lost too much blood.

It must be done.

I will see you in Valhalla.

I shook the fog away.

Using the last of my strength, I grabbed my father's axe, slowly lifting the immensely heavy weapon. It was now my turn to wield it, and none would be heavier than its first swing.

Lurching forward, I screamed as I rushed the man who had made me who I was. Tears streaked my eyes as I closed in for the killing blow. "FATHER!"

The room exploded into a bright flash.

Stunned, my head rang and I blinked at the spots blinding my vision. The axe wavered over my head.

"Son." The words were barely a whisper, but I heard them.

Diverting my blow, I smashed the axe into the rock beside him.

He had dropped my axe and stared at me, a sadness in his eyes, but recognition.

I fell to my knees tears streaking the dirt on my face. "I almost killed you," I said gasping for breath.

"Run you dogs!" Flo screamed at the voldak scrambling to flee.

Caspian, blood soaked but still breathing, slid against the nearby wall. The demon had vanished.

Emerging from the side tunnel, Kole strolled out with Baba Yaga's head dangling from his left hand. "What did I miss?"

My father knelt beside me and grabbed my shoulders. "I am proud of you. You did not falter."

Meeting his gaze, I wiped my face and said, "I thought I failed you."

It was then I noticed the red swirling within his eyes. The mark of the voldak. "No. No, it can't be." I didn't want to believe it. Not after everything that had happened.

Seeming to know what I spoke of, he sighed and stood. "The witch turned me a day ago."

"Holemgeiir, you joke," Flo said with a weak smile. "You are no mindless beast."

"No, he's something else." Kole dropped Baba Yaga's head by our feet. "He is a vampire—a higher level voldak. He still has the thirst, but he has full control of his mind. It was the demon who had him under a spell."

It was all too much for my mind to take. Rubbing the sides of my forehead, I tried to calm the rage and confusion of my thoughts. What was I going to do now?

"Please, wake up." Danica's soft cries shattered my own worries, and I was on my feet and racing to Agna.

Danica sat beside Agna who lay on the ground.

"Agna." Leaning over her, I whispered her name and kissed her head.

Though she lay still, her chest moved with life. My heart crushed under the weight of my sleeping beauty. What was wrong?

"It was the witch," Danica cried, her voice cracking with each word. "She cast some spell and I can't break it."

I turned to call for Kole, but he was already kneeling next to me. He ran a hand across her cheek, his brow furrowed. "I am no witch, but I sense the darkness on her."

"How do we get rid of it?" As soon as I asked the question, I knew the answer.

All the fire in Kole's eyes disappeared as he gathered Agna in his arms. "I don't know if we can. Baba Yaga is the strongest witch I know." He kissed the top of Agna's head. "I am sorry, *krasavitza moya.*"

"No. No!" I jumped to my feet, swaying as the blood from my wounds dizzied my mind. "I won't lose her."

Everyone quieted, and only Danica's sobs echoed through the cavern.

Caspian's face paled to the point of death, Fey barely breathed in the corner, and the girl who had my heart lay in a deep sleep. Kole may not know how to help them, but I did.

Quickly, I ripped my shirt and tied it tight around my arm, stopping the blood.

"The willow," I said, taking Agna from Kole. With her in

my arms, I glanced around at our broken team. "There is an ancient tree. Powerful, more powerful than any being I've encountered."

A spark flashed in Kole's eyes. "I'll take the wolf."

Flo wrapped an arm around Caspian's waist. "I've got the priest, but we need to hurry. He's lost too much blood."

Father reached over and touched my shoulder. "I cannot go with you."

"Father, you are not like them. You can stay with us."

"I cannot. You have done well, my boy." He squeezed my shoulder. "We will meet again, of that I am certain."

Flo and my father stared at one another, and I wondered what they were thinking. They had grown up together, fought side by side, and left our home across the seas for a new life in Novgorod.

"For being dead," Flo said, "you look rather well."

Father smiled. "Watch my boy."

Flo's face hardened as all the jokes he had vanished with the seriousness of the moment. "Aye. You kill as many of those bastards as you can, and I will see you at the gates."

Father nodded, and picked up his axe. "That is a promise I can keep."

If Agna hadn't been in my arms, stuck in a world of darkness, I would have argued with my father to stay. To find a way for us to be together. But I knew it would take more than convincing with my father, and I didn't have the time. Not now. Too many of my loved ones were dying.

Dawn broke above the thin trees as we left the cave. Sunlight lit the dismal swamp in hues of orange and pinks.

We were too broken and injured to muck our way through mud. Thankfully, Kole led us a different way out, longer but the ground was solid.

Danica used a salve on my arm to stop the bleeding. With Agna in my arms, the cut throbbed and my arm tingled. If it wasn't for the adrenaline pulsing through me, keeping me sharp and focused, I wouldn't have had the strength to carry her all that way.

When the giant leaves of the willow came in to view, relief flooded through me. My eyes watered from the pain coursing through my tired body, and I hoped the ancient tree would heal them all.

We stepped onto the bright green grass. I swayed, almost dropping Agna.

Danica slipped her arms underneath Agna. "Let me take her, please."

I nodded, and Danica carried Agna to the base of the ancient tree. My knees gave way, and I toppled to the ground, breathing fast. The cool grass invited me to sleep, but I couldn't, not until I knew they were all safe. That they were all alive.

My vision winked in and out. Spots blocked my view of Agna's precious face. Caspian, Fey, and Agna all lay beneath the ancient tree. Wind rushed around the glade, rustling the leaves. The Will-O-Wisps danced around the three of them, covering their bodies in a blanket of white. Flo spoke to me, but his voice muffled in my head.

Stay with me, Agna.

With Father gone, Fey dying, and Agna stuck in a sleepless

world, the worry and fear weighted so heavy, no matter how many times I blinked the sleepiness away, it rushed over me, forcing my eyes closed.

Agna faded from my sight as fatigue won the battle.

Fight for me, Agna. Don't give up.

34

Tiny feathers tickled my skin. "Stop that," I giggled, rubbing my eyes open. Little wisps of white flew around me. My skin tingled and my throat ached for a sip of water.

"It worked. It worked!" Danica threw herself around me, crushing the breath out of my lungs. "Thank, Perun!"

Kole smirked, and I had never been so grateful to see him. "Welcome back, *krasavitza moya*. I thought I had lost you for a moment." His black eyes sparkled crimson, and he leaned over to kiss my hand. "That's almost twice, now."

"What happened? Why are we at the willow?"

Cloudiness filled my head, and I tried to think of the last thing I remembered. "Yaya."

Danica let go, and wiped her face. Her eyes were red as if she had cried for days. "It's a long, painful story, and one we can discuss when you're better."

She slid back, and that's when I saw him lying on the ground.

"Folkvarr!" I shoved my sister aside in my haste to get to him.

"Don't worry," Kole said. "Your Viking lives."

I brushed the hair off his face. He breathed in and out, and though I so desperately wanted to wake him, I couldn't. "Tell me what happened."

"What do you remember?" Danica refused to meet my eyes, and I knew the two of us still had a lot to talk about, privately.

"I remember being taken by that demon then being in that terrifying cave. Where is the witch?"

"Dead," Kole said. Fire burned in his eyes, matching the hue of his dark auburn hair. "Along with the demon. Your priest friend almost lost his life destroying it."

Caspian leaned against the tree trunk, sleeping, his left shoulder wrapped in cloth. Fey lay beside him, blood covering his coat, but breathing.

"His arm . . . is it?"

"Gone." Flo came out of the woods carrying a horn. "Here, water."

He handed me the horn and I drank it quickly. The cool water soaking my parched throat. I wiped the drops from my mouth and handed it back. "Thank you."

He nodded and his gaze went to Folkvarr. "He'll be happy to know you live."

There were so many emotions running through me, and one beautiful, hopeful thought. "If the witch is dead, we can save his father. Maybe the magic is gone."

Every single one of them avoided my gaze.

"Tell me." If something happened, I needed to know.

"You've just woken up, rest." Danica gave me a smile, but I wouldn't be swayed.

"Flo?" While I could always count on Kole to be honest, the leshii took this moment to be silent.

"Aye," Flo crouched beside me. "The witch is dead, and the remaining voldak scattered. As for Holemgeiir, that is another story."

In the sunlit glade, Flo told me of the horrors of the cave. How Holemgeiir had been turned and Folkvarr forced to fight him. Tears ran freely when Flo spoke of the moment he knew Folkvarr would have to strike, how he himself didn't know if he would've been able to make that final blow to a man he called brother. Peace covered Folkvarr as he slept, and my heart hurt at what he went through. To have to kill your own father.

We failed.

A snap sounded from my left and I caught Kole peering at me beneath those dark lashes. I made a deal with the devil and it was for nothing. All of it, for nothing! What would happen now? Would Folkvarr stay true to his word and marry me? Even after everything that happened? And Kole, I still had no idea how I could break the oath I made.

Flo finished the story. Knowing Holemgeiir still had his mind, gave me a little peace. Though, I knew Folkvarr would never rest knowing his father walked the lands, undead.

Folkvarr moaned and Flo walked away to give us privacy.

"Folkvarr." I gently rubbed my hand across his cheek, not wanting to wake him up, but unable to keep my hands away from him.

His eyes fluttered open. "Agna?"

I nodded as a thousand flutters filled my stomach.

"Thank the gods!" He bolted upright and hugged me, crushing me with kiss after kiss. He dug his hands into my hair, pulling me closer to him, deepening the kiss as if he needed my air to breathe.

My body responded to his touch, aching for more, desperate for us to be alone in this glade. Yet, I could sense my sister's gaze on my back.

Folkvarr pulled away, glancing behind me. "I'm sorry. I know your sister—"

"I don't care," I said, tugging his shirt. "Let her watch."

His lip curled into a grin. "No, I want you all to myself, alone." He whispered the words into my lips, and kissed me one last time before breaking away to check on Caspian.

Dusting the grass and dirt off my clothes, I breathed in deep, trying to settle my racing heart. Danica stood, and with her head lowered, shoulders sagging, she walked to meet me. My sister and I had much to discuss. So much I almost didn't have the strength to hear it. We stood at arm's length, and every moment she refused to speak, I wondered why I was even giving her a chance to.

"Forgive me." She never lifted her head. "I missed them so much. I thought . . ." She shook her head as if the words needed to be loosed from her mind. "She said if I helped, she would bring them back."

"Is that why you did this? To bring our parents back?"

Her shoulders shook. "I miss them. Every day. The pain never leaves." She glanced at me with watery eyes, red from crying, and filled with a hopelessness that broke my heart.

I wrapped my arms around her and let my little sister cry into me. "I miss them too."

She sobbed and I rubbed her back. I knew this was her fault, that all of it was hers to blame, yet I couldn't hate her. I shared her pain. It made sense why Papa showed that night and why she reacted with wonder. Baba Yaga had promised her a miracle, and she believed it.

Part of me felt to blame. I knew she took our parents' death hard, but this past year she wore a smile instead of a bitter frown. We spent our days in laughter, and running through the woods, playing with the mist at our feet.

How did I not see the anguish she hid?

Danica's sobs lightened, and only when I heard her sniffles end, did I let her go. "I'm sorry."

She shook her head. "No. I'm sorry."

Folkvarr sat in the grass petting Fey's head and whispering to him. Caspian rose and chatted with Kole, though there seemed to be a bit of annoyance in his words. I didn't think our Christian friend thought much of Kole, but then he shook his hand.

Danica grasped my hand. "Everything will be okay. You'll see."

I leaned my head against her shoulder, holding her close, thinking on her words. No matter what, I would never stop fighting for my friends or the people I loved.

As I glanced at Folkvarr, his gaze met mine.

Danica was right. Everything would be okay.

35

Before the day ended, we left the glade and headed back to the settlement. Agna insisted we return quickly to Yaya's. In all the chaos, we had left the poor woman to rot on the ground. I offered to handle the matter myself, but Agna and Danica both refused. Yaya was their grandmother and their burden to bear.

Agna and Danica walked arm in arm ahead of me.

While I knew it was wrong to be selfish in this moment, all I could think about was what would happen next. With my father gone, I had to return home. I couldn't leave my brothers, not at their age, and my mother? Mother would take the news hard. I would tell them Father died in battle, for in my eyes he did.

Yaya's hut came into view and a woman sat on the ground next to a body covered with a blanket. Lew off to the side, chewing grass.

"Aunt Jasna!" Agna screamed, and when her aunt turned, all three women ran at once.

They crashed into the ground, hugging, crying, and holding each other.

"My girls. My girls." Jasna kissed their faces and held a chin in each hand. "I have been worried, terrified for you." She squeezed them against her chest.

"Yaya's gone." Agna sobbed and Jasna rocked her and Danica in her arms.

"It's my fault," Danica added. "I thought the coven could help."

Jasna's eyes went wide and she broke away from Agna to grab Danica at arm's length. "What have you done? I taught you the old ways to give you *peace* not destruction."

"I'm sorry. I didn't mean for this." Danica cried so loud I could feel her heart breaking with each sob.

"What's done is done," Jasna said softly. "We must move forward, the best we can."

This time Agna pulled away. Her gaze went to me, and I knew she was thinking the same thing.

What happens to us?

Flo helped Caspian back to the settlement where he could rest. I stayed to help with Yaya's burial. While the women went inside, I gathered branches to make Yaya a raft. Jasna insisted we take her to the water and release her spirit there. I worked through the rest of the night, until Agna came out to stop me.

"You should rest." She handed me a bowl of soup. "Eat."

"Thank you." I drank the warm mushroom soup, thankful to have a bit of food in my belly. The ache in my head dulled.

"Here." She handed me a smaller bowl full of fresh water.

She took a blanket and laid it out on the ground and took another one to drape over her crossed legs. "It's strange with her gone. Yaya has been the one constant in my life. I don't know how I'll survive without her."

Dropping the bowl, I moved closer. She lifted the blanket and placed it over both of us. I grabbed her hand and squeezed it.

"I know how you feel. While my father is still alive, he is an abomination to our way of life, and that is worse than death."

Her lips trembled as she met my gaze. "I'm so sorry. After everything." She bit her lip.

I would not let this burden fall on her.

I shushed her with my mouth, forcing the conversation to end. She fell into me, opening her arms, and tugging me closer. With a gentle movement, I laid her back and kissed the soft skin on her neck.

The need to be with her grew until the heat almost made me lose control. She teased me with playful touches, and when she bit my bottom lip, I wanted to cave. Agna would be my wife, and I would wait until then. With a final kiss, I broke our connection and laid on my back.

"That's it?" she said, pursing her lips at me.

I smiled. "For tonight, yes. I would not dishonor you, especially while your aunt is a stone's throw away."

Agna rolled on top of me and placed her hands beside my face. "I don't care who is inside. Will you not have me?"

With a quick switch, I rolled her under me. "I will have you every night, and every day."

Her cheeks flushed red and she tugged at my shirt, drawing me near.

"But tonight, I'm going to hold you." I grazed my thumb across her cheek. "I love you, and though I want you, in many different ways, I am saving us for our wedding night."

"I still haven't told Aunt Jasna."

"It doesn't matter." I moved to slide behind Agna and grabbed her in my arms. "I don't care what anyone says. You are my wife. We'll sort out the rest later."

Lew bleated as Fey trotted out of the woods to curl beside us on the ground. With Agna in my arms, our peculiar pets next to us, I knew everything would be fine, as long as we were together.

36

uietly, I slipped out of the house, searching the settlement for any signs of Folkvarr or Fey. Nothing but the gray mist and the wind rustling the leaves. After Yaya's burial, Aunt Jasna told me my betrothed had returned to Kiev, the deal off. Apparently they had ventured to Yaya's and that's when Aunt Jasna found her body. The merchant's son cared only about the "arrangement" and Aunt Jasna nearly drove her sword through him. Folkvarr had proven his intentions, and she knew I would be cared for. She didn't give me her blessing, but she promised she would not stand in the way.

It seemed everything was slipping into place. Except the one big secret, I still hadn't shared with Folkvarr.

I had to find Kole and make him undo our agreement. With quick steps, I hurried into the forest, no longer afraid of the voldak that used to roam these woods. Once I passed Yaya's, and the long stream that led to the sacred willow, I stopped and called out.

It had been three days since I last saw him, and I prayed to Perun he was in the area. "Kole!"

Wind whispered back, blowing my apron. Little slivers of sunlight peeked through the mist, slowly waking the forest from its night slumber. I wrapped my arms around my chest, shivering from the cold.

"Kole!"

"No reason to shout, *lyubimaya.*"

I jumped at the sound of his voice behind me. Spinning around, I stepped back, putting distance between me and those coal-fire eyes. "We need to speak."

The casual grin on his face faded. "I know what you're going to ask, and the answer is no."

"But, why? After everything I did, we did, how can you still bind me to this?" Hurt, fear, and sadness ached deep within my bones.

"My beauty." He glided forward, lifting his hand to cup my chin. "I know love when I see it. Powerful and unending. But no matter how strong your love is, our bond is made. Once a deal is struck, neither you nor I have the power to break it."

Tears welled in my eyes. "Then I'll just stay with Folkvarr. We'll run away. You'll never find us." I pulled away from Kole, folding my arms and meeting his intense stare.

"If only it were as simple as that." He sighed and ran a hand through his wild hair. "The bond links us, and in time you will be drawn to me. A desire so overpowering, you cannot control it, nor break it."

My heart stopped at his words. "What are you saying?"

"Your love will not be enough to save you. You *will* come to me."

"No." I shook my head, my whole body trembled. "No. I won't. We're to marry! I'll never leave him. You're a liar!"

"Agna."

It was the first time he'd ever said my name. The truth that the situation was so dire he could no longer joke broke me. Tears slipped one after the other, a waterfall of despair I couldn't stop.

"I am sorry," he whispered, suddenly by my side and holding me. "I've grown fond of you, and I wouldn't see you hurt, but this is beyond us."

"So, I will fall for you, leave my husband, and you will pity me forever?" The words fumbled out amidst the tears.

"No. The bond works both ways." He leaned his head against mine. "We will fall for each other, but I promise you this, I will not call on the old magic to force you here. You will have your time with the Viking."

Closing my eyes, I pictured Folkvarr's face. The face of the boy who had protected me, fought for me, and loved me. How could I ever stop the feelings I had for him? The thought of leaving him, unable to stop it, terrified me.

Kole held me in his arms, silent, my aching sobs filling the forest with a somber melody.

"Go, *lyubimaya.*" He kissed the top of my head and released me from his grasp.

I nodded, my voice sore and harsh from crying. With a quick bow, he shifted into a bird and flew away.

Sadness filled my steps as I journeyed back home and

thought of how I could break an unbreakable bond.

***

"What is it? What are you hiding?"

Folkvarr held on my arms as if the mist would steal me away. After everything we'd endured, how could I tell him we could never be. I could never be his wife. The pain was too much.

We sat on a hill, a blanket draped over our shoulders, protecting us from the night's chill. All day I had tried to avoid Folkvarr, unsure of what to say, but when he requested a night under the stars, my heart could not resist.

I wrapped my hand around his. "I will not deny the feelings I have nor how much I pray that we could be, but we live in separate worlds." My voice croaked, and I refused to look at him. "I cannot ask you to stay, and I cannot leave my home."

"Don't do this." His grip slightly tightened and he touched his head to mine. "There is no god nor man who can ever separate us. Do you not feel it?" He touched the side of my cheek and the tears slipped, slowly, painfully.

"I do," I whispered, holding him and regretting the bargain I had struck.

"Tell me why." Folkvarr held my face within his hands, searching my eyes for answers I was terrified to give. "What has changed? Please." The way he said please, desperate for an answer.

"Kiss me," I said, not wanting to discuss anything more. "Kiss me as if you will never see me again."

He pressed his lips against mine, crushing me with the touch of his love, and pushing me far away into another world. "I cannot bear to be without you. The mere thought of it destroys me." His lips trailed to my face, to my neck, to all the places I wish he'd never touched.

"Tell me, why." He gripped me tighter, kissed me harder, forcing me to give him answers.

I loved him.

And he deserved the truth.

I released the fear burning inside. Folkvarr would find a way to stop Kole. Together, we would be unbreakable.

"Folkvarr," I whispered, pulling him back to our world. "Folkvarr, listen."

Pulling me into his chest, he ran his hand across my neck and into my hair. "Speak."

While he gently stroked the strands of my hair, I gazed at the hand I held. "When I summoned the leshii, I had to make a deal."

Folkvarr's hand stopped. "What did you do?"

Gripping his hand tighter, I found the words I fought so hard to hold in. "In order for Kole to show me the rusalki palace, I had to give him one human soul . . . mine."

Silence floated around us, but Folkavarr's chest heaved up and down. He gripped the side of my arm, hugging me tighter. "He will not have you."

"But—"

"No one will take you."

"It's more than that." I buried my face into Folkvarr's chest, holding onto him as if this truth would rip me away this instant. "The bond is magical, and in time, I will go to him. He said it's unstoppable and there is no way to break it, even if he wanted to."

"And you believe him?"

"I do."

The muscles of Folkvarr's jaw clenched and his gaze drifted over the grassy hill and out to the sky. "We will find a way," he finally said, turning back to me. He shifted his body, pulling me up into his lap and holding my face with his hands. "We will break this curse, or let Odin take me now."

His lips landed on mine, sealing the promise with a kiss. I didn't know whether we would find a way to undo the deal I had made, but I knew Folkvarr would stay by my side until the very end.

And for now, that was enough.

THE END

ACKNOWLEDGEMENTS

Thank you for reading my beloved Viking tale. When I decided to write a novel about Vikings, I wanted to create a villain that could scare them ... and what scares a Viking? Not reaching Valhalla.

My favorite part of writing this story was the research. Thank you to Lisa Gus who swapped many emails with me on proper Russian language and for my girl Janelle Howard on finding out the proper spelling of RubaKHA.

I wanted this story to have a historical focal point. I choose the years surrounded the Varangian chieftain of the Rus', Rurik. It was during that time the Vikings began trading. While some of the aspects are close to history, this is still a fantasy tale.

Much love to Marlene Moss. After eight years of friendship, she still loves to help me out and provide outstanding feedback. I don't know where I would be in my writing career. Thank you!

For those of you who don't know, my husband plays a big role in my writing. Not only did he hand drawn the wolf and ram for the chapter headings, but he's an extremely talented writer who takes my fight scenes and catapults them to the next level. Our writing is so in sync, you can't tell when one of us ends and one begins. I can't wait for us to do a full coauthored novel. The world just isn't ready for it.

While this is a stand alone novel, I LOVE these characters and this world. Plus, can we really leave things as they are?

•258•

GLOSSARY

•259•

Here are a few words found throughout the story with a little more clarity.

Leshii: Spirit of the woodlands

Rusalka: Magical water maidens who lure men to their watery graves

Domovoi (Grandfather): A male house spirit

Perun: The highest god in Slavic mythology

Lyubimaya: Beloved

Vnuchenka: Granddaughter

Krasavitza moya: My beauty

RubaKHa: Traditional Russian linen shirt

About the Author

USA Today Bestselling author, Eliza Tilton, graduated from Dowling College with a BA in Visual Communications. When she's not arguing with excel at her day job, chasing after four kids, playing video games, or writing, she's getting her post-baby body back and inspiring people on the way. Her YA Fantasy, *The Daath Chronicles*, is published by Curiosity Quills Press.

Read More from Eliza Tilton

http://elizatilton.com/